Respectfully,

CMC Dixon

Riain Wacx

D1528529

Respectfully, CMC Dixon

©2014 Riain Wacx

ISBN-13: 978-1500462444

ISBN-10: 1500462446

First Printing: 2014

Covers by Rogenna

http://www.rogennabrewer.com

Respectfully,

CMC Dixon

Respectfully, CMC Dixon

Acknowledgements

To all our brave men and women in uniform, past and present--thank you for your courage and sacrifice.

Erin P. and Jerika F.- Thank you for your hours of helping me make sense of some of the ideas for this book and your friendship! Without it, this would have never came to be!

Amanda E.-I'm so glad someone else understands my anger issues with stupid people! You've been invaluable as a friend and a venting post! Thank you!

All my friends and family who have stood by me through the years, supported me and put up with me scribbling down notes when I probably shouldn't have. Thank you for putting up with me.

My "mentor", Rogenna-Thank you for the amazing work you have done for me, the endless emails back and forth and guidance on writing. Your wisdom, friendship and support over the years means so much to me. Thank you!

My Navy family that started with Great Lakes, U.S.S Dwight D. Eisenhower, Portsmouth Naval Hospital and into the Seabee community (among other commands), thank you all for your service, your friendship and your inspiration.

CMSC(Ret.)Mike K.- Thank you for being a man that my husband and I respect and look up to. It's an honor knowing you Sir, hope you and the missus like the promotion!

Bailey C.- My editor, writing buddy, whip cracker. Thanks for being there for me and helping me get through this! Can't wait to do the next one with you! Love you girl!

My children- Bubs and Squeak- you guys keep me going every day. I'm so glad you were little the last time Daddy deployed, I don't think we could make it now that you're older. Momma loves you both!

Last, but certainly not least—My husband CM2 Wacx. My Seabee, my hero in cammies. We made it through Iraq, even when shit hit the fan. Without your input Logan could have never been. Thank you for supporting me through this, even when I wanted to give up. You're my strength this last decade, let's put in for another ten eh? I love you.

To all the Ann's who are wailing for their Logan to return home- thank you for your sacrifice.

Respectfully, CMC Dixon

Explanation of Terms Used:

HMC- Hospital Corpsmen are medical professionals who provide health care to service people and their families. They serve as pharmacy technicians, medical technicians, nurse's aides, physician's or dentist's assistants, battlefield medics, and more. All work falls into several categories: first aid and minor surgery, patient transportation, patient care, prescriptions and laboratory work, food service inspections, and clerical duties. The rank is E-7, commonly known as Chief Petty Officer, considered upper management. This rating exists in all aspects and communities of the Navy. Lower ranks (in descending order) are known as HM1, HM2, HM3. They are commonly called Corpsman or Doc.

CMC-Construction Mechanics maintain many types of construction machinery including; buses, dump trucks, bulldozers, rollers, cranes, backhoes, and pile drivers. They work on gasoline and diesel engines and transmissions. They also repair electrical, hydraulic, pneumatic and steering systems. This rating is given to the Seabee community, and does not exist outside of it. The rank is E-7, commonly known as Chief Petty Officer, considered upper management. Lower ranks (in descending order) are known as CM1, CM2, CM3, CMCN, CMCA, CMCR.

YNSN- This rank is low on the chain of command coming in at E-2. Yeomen are the enlisted Navy clerk whose duties are mostly clerical.

MTVR- Medium Tactical Vehicle Replacement (MTVR) or 7-Ton, is an all-wheel drive all-terrain vehicle used by the United States Marine Corps and United States Navy.

MRAP- Mine-Resistant Ambush Protected vehicles are armored fighting vehicles used by various armed forces, whose designed purpose is surviving improvised explosive device (IED) attacks and ambushes.

CASH- A Combat Action Support Hospital-CASH is a type of modern United States military field hospital. The CASH is transportable by aircraft and trucks and is normally delivered to the Corps Support Area in standard military-owned Demountable Containers-similar to cargo containers. Once transported, it is assembled by the staff into a tent hospital to treat patients. Depending upon the operational environment, a CASH might also treat civilians and wounded enemy soldiers. The CASH is the successor to the Mobile Army Surgical Hospital (MASH).

NMCB- Naval Mobile Construction Battalion. A community within the U.S. Navy that consists of Seabees and their specific unit. The NMCB is a mobile command that travels all over the world to complete the mission at hand. The Seabees build, repair and fight when necessary.

Seabees- A Seabee is a member of the United States Navy Construction Battalion (CB). The word "Seabee" comes from initials "CB". The Seabees have a history of building bases, bulldozing and paving thousands of miles of roadway and airstrips, and accomplishing a myriad of other construction projects in a wide variety of military theaters dating back to World War II.

MRE- The Meal, Ready-to-Eat – commonly known as the MRE – is a self-contained, individual field ration in lightweight packaging bought by the United States military for its service members for use in combat or other field conditions where organized food facilities are not available.

DADT- "Don't ask, don't tell" was the official United States policy on service by gays and lesbians in the military instituted by the Clinton Administration in February 28, 1994, when Department of Defense Directive 1304.26 issued on December 21, 1993, took effect, lasting until September 20, 2011. The policy prohibited military personnel from discriminating against or harassing closeted homosexual or bisexual service members or applicants, while barring openly gay, lesbian, or bisexual persons from military service.

NEX-Navy Exchange. The on base version of a shopping mall. Only service members have access to it, as it offers items at a significantly lower price than stores offbase. Most Navy bases have at least one, if not two. They are usually paired up with the commissary, uniform shop and gas station.

TBI- Traumatic Brain Injury-also known as intracranial injury, occurs when an external force traumatically injures the brain. TBI can be classified based on severity, mechanism (closed or penetrating head injury), or other features (e.g., occurring in a specific location or over a widespread area).

IED- is a homemade bomb constructed and deployed in ways other than in conventional military action. It may be constructed of conventional military explosives, such as an artillery round, attached to a detonating mechanism. Roadside bombs are a common use of IEDs.

VA- Veteran's Administration. Commonly refers to the hospital system for veterans.

Chapter One

Ann Stranahan reached up to pluck one of the colorful cards off the beautiful Christmas tree that stood in the foyer of the church she attended. The tree stood six feet tall; the lights twinkled like stars around the metallic baubles and garland that adorned the boughs. An angel topped the tree, giving it an ethereal appearance in the stone darkness of the foyer. A few cards still sparsely hung on the branches, as if people just forgot they were there. Ann felt terrible for the last two cards that hung on the tree, making a mental note to take them next Sunday if they were still there. June Betzner always had the Holidays for Heroes cards up every year, but this year was the first year Ann felt compelled to take one of the cards.

Ann had meant to take one every year prior, but she usually ducked out early from the end of the service to beat the crowd out of the parking lot to get home to study. She tucked the card into her purse, looking for an open spot in the pews for the morning services at Our Lady of Mount Carmel. In the quiet of the congregation offering up their personal prayers to God, Ann felt herself relaxing. Her thoughts shifted to the card in her purse as she knelt down to pray; Ann grew up in the all American farm family, she had always respected the service members who spent months away from their families to protect the American people. That was how her family was: the kind that said grace before meals, went to church on Sunday and had strong family ties. That was the Stranahan family in a nutshell, American as apple pie.

Ann heard the first few bars of the processional begin; she came up slowly from her knees to watch the altar boys light the candles and the priest bow before the altar. The service passed quickly for Ann, Sunday Mass was autopilot for her after so many years of going with her family, her faith was really becoming habitual but she couldn't just stop it. Ann scooted out to the parking lot; clicking the button on her key ring, hearing the engine turn over and the lights flash on her Ford

Explorer. She hated the cold of New York, but was slowly adjusting to it since this was her sixth year at New York Medical College. Another full year and Ann would graduate with her Doctorate in Medicine and would be able to license and practice anywhere she wanted to in the nation.

Pulling into the drive through lane of the local Starbucks, Ann ordered her usual venti chai latte and waited for her turn at the receiving window. Digging through her purse to get her wallet, Ann's fingers grazed over the card from the tree at church. Pulling it out with her wallet, Ann flipped the card over and read the neatly typed sticker attached to the card:

CMC Dixon, Logan W.

NMCB 17 / Alfa Company

Camp Fallujah, Iraq

FPO-AE 09532-7415

Ann's breath caught in her throat, Iraq was where the heavy fighting was from what the news portrayed lately. Between the IED's and the terrorist attacks, Americans were in a precarious situation in the desert that seemed to have no reprieve. A car honking startled Ann out of her concerned state, the card with the name slipping through her fingers falling to the floorboard.

"Damn it." she muttered, pulling up to the window to exchange her money for the chai that was hanging out in the cold air. Ann drank deep from the cup in her hand, the rich flavor of the milk and tea distracting her thoughts of CMC Logan Dixon in Iraq. Unlocking the front door of her apartment; Ann tossed her purse onto the couch as she shucked out of her winter coat and heels. She hummed to herself as she changed into a pair of jeans and a t-shirt, washing the makeup off her face. Ann sighed at the feeling of her clean face, pulling her hair up into a high ponytail.

"Damn it, I forgot that card out in the truck." Ann huffed as she grabbed her keys off the kitchen bar, running out the door in her bare feet. Her toes crunched over the powder soft snow, Ann's hand jerked the truck door open, seeing the bent corner of the card underneath the driver's seat. She smoothed the card out before shutting the truck door; the snowflakes falling into her hair as she hightailed it to the door of her apartment, the card held tight to her chest.

Ann set the card down at her computer desk, pouring herself a glass of ice water before she started in on her cardiology homework that was due for tomorrow's class. Staring at the knowledge module of a heart pumping blood, Ann's eyes darted to the card again. She was supposed to be doing tests with different drugs on the online heart and logging her findings. But that wasn't happening with her curiosity getting the best of her; Ann saved her answers, logging out of the school's online learning site. Ann brought up the Google search engine, typing in NMCB 17 Alfa Company, getting a few good hits. The first was a Navy website, that clued her into that

Logan was part of the Navy, but what would he be doing in the desert of Iraq? Wasn't everyone in the Navy stationed on ships at sea? She took a long drink of her glass of water before pulling up the next site on the list, which happened to be the battalion's public website.

Ann read through the history of how the battalion was created and that it was home based in Fort Carson, CO. There were pictures of the Commanding Officer, a Lieutenant Sean Kelly, who looked about fifty and knew the meaning of a hard day's work, but no pictures of what they were doing in Iraq and definitely no pictures of Logan. Not that she cared what he looked like really, she just liked to have a face that went with the name on the card. Looking through the website she learned that NMCB 17 was a Naval Mobile Construction Battalion, and were affectionately known as "Seabees". The Seabee motto explained a lot, "We Build, We Fight." So Logan was part of a group who was moving around building and fighting in Iraq, which made Ann feel better that he was doing more than just fighting. Ann couldn't find much else on the website, she figured she could send a letter and ask Logan questions about what he did. That would be the most direct way of getting information about what he did and what he was involved in.

Ann clicked through a few more websites about what was acceptable to send to troops in Iraq, finding that pork products and anything pornographic was prohibited. Like she was going to send anything pornographic to a complete stranger-- that was just disturbing. Most of the sites said travel size bathroom items, baby wipes, books, cd's and homemade baked goods were always appreciated and welcome to deployed troops. She decided then that she would bake two dozen of her mother's famous chocolate chip cookies and send them off to Logan with a letter explaining who she was and how she came across his address. If it was her in his shoes, she would love to get a box of homemade cookies and a note of appreciation from someone in the States when she was so far from home.

Ann closed the laptop; grabbing her notebook out of her backpack and a pen, lying down on her bed with a blank page in front of her. Her mother always said if you were going to write a letter to someone that you should always handwrite it, that it carried more of yourself with it and it was more personal. Ann quickly scribbled down what she needed to make the cookies, thinking she would go over to the C-Town and pick up the ingredients to make cookies today. She knew she could get the box out in the morning mail before her 10am class, that way she wouldn't forget about it being in her truck during class.

Ann caught herself writing the letter without much thought put to it, words filling up the new blank page in front of her.

Dear CMC Dixon,

Hello, how are you? My name is Ann Stranahan and I came across your address on the Holidays for Heroes tree at my local church. I thought I would write to you and thank you for your selfless sacrifice to serve our country. I have the upmost respect for you doing what you do, it takes a special kind of person to give up so much for strangers.

I can't imagine what it is like over there in Iraq, your family must be worried about you and miss you terribly. What is it that you do over there? What is your day like? Do you like what you're doing over there? I watch the news nightly, but I'm sure what I see on it is nothing like what you experience.

I hope you enjoy the cookies that are in this box, I baked them using my mother's blue ribbon winning recipe. I would love to correspond with you if that's okay? I know it sounds cheesy, like being pen pals when you're kids, but I'd really appreciate it if I could know that you got this package and you're okay. I wish you all the best, and hope to hear from you soon.

Sincerely,

Ann

      Ann sighed at the words on the page in her flowing handwriting. She really had no idea what to say to someone she didn't know, but felt she should say something to. Ann was sure the man had a family here in the States, but she didn't see any harm in sending him a box of goodies every once in a while with a friendly letter. The websites said that deployed service members loved getting mail from "back home" since many didn't have families to go home to. She really couldn't imagine not having a family to come home from war to; her family was such an integral part of her life that Krista called or texted almost daily and her mama and daddy called once a week to check in with her. Family was the cornerstone in her life, and at some point Ann hoped to have a family of her own after she graduated and got settled in her career as a doctor.

Getting up from the bed, Ann grabbed a pair of socks out of her drawer, slipping into her boots and pulling a heavy hoodie over her t-shirt. The C-Town was just a few miles away, there wasn't any point in putting on her heavy jacket and purse. Roaming up and down the aisles of the grocery store proved to be detrimental to Ann's bank account, she ended up with more in her cart than was on her list. That was how it always was when Ann went to the store hungry, forgetting to get lunch after church.

She cringed swiping her debit card at the checkout, knowing that she would have to make what was in the cart last the next three weeks until her work study money came in for the month. Ann carried the groceries into her one bedroom apartment, putting everything away but the things she needed to make the cookies. She set the oven to 325 and set about making the dough. The dough came together just like Ann remembered it when she made it with her mother, doling it out in clumps onto the parchment lined cookie sheets.

Ann's cellphone rang in her purse, distracting her from the cookies baking in the oven. Ann smiled when she saw it was her mother calling, clicking the button and crooking the phone in between her shoulder and neck.

"Hi Mama, how are you and Daddy?" Ann greeted her mother with a happy chipper to her voice.

"We're good baby, how are you? You sound happy." Ann instantly relaxed at her mother's thick southern accent, it wasn't something she heard often up in New York.

"I'm good, I'm making your cookies for a Holidays for Heroes project I picked up at church today. It's an address of a deployed service member that I can send care packages to, so I thought he would appreciate some cookies." Ann felt her smile at telling her mother what she was working on.

"That's wonderful honey, where is this young man deployed to?" Annette was pleased yet concerned for the destination of the cookies her youngest was making to send through the mail.

"He's in the Navy and he's in Iraq Mama. I'm sort of worried for him being over there with everything I've seen on the news lately." Annette knew that Ann had a good heart; it would be out of character if she wasn't worried for this complete stranger, it was just how she was.

"Well I'm sure he is okay sweetheart, and I'm sure he will enjoy your cookies. I'll leave you to it then before you burn them. We love you and miss you, looking forward to you coming home for Christmas in a few weeks." Annette's words brought Ann to the present, making her realize that her cookies were indeed burning.

"Gotta go Mama, love you and Daddy." Ann hung up quickly, sprinting for the small kitchen to pull out the pan of cookies. Sliding them onto cooling racks; Ann realized that she had saved them just in the nick of time, a minute or two more and the cookies would have been trash can fodder. Sighing with relief Ann put the rest of the dough onto a cool cookie sheet and set a timer. She wasn't about to be embarrassed by sending somewhat burnt cookies to Iraq, and she wasn't going to start a fresh batch just to end up eating the dough herself.

With the cookies cooled, boxed up with an address written on the top of the box and her homework done, Ann curled up with a book that her friend Leah had loaned her weeks ago. Ann had been promising to read it, but hadn't found time until now. Lost in the world of dwarves and elves, Ann tucked the card with Logan's address in as a bookmark before finding something for dinner.

Chapter Two

Construction Mechanic Chief Logan Dixon heard someone calling his name across the din of shop, tossing the wrench in his hand onto the concrete floor underneath the MTVR he was working on. Wiping sweat from his face before wiping his hands on the shop rag hanging out of his back pocket, he sought out the person calling his name. The heat in Iraq made him sweat; his brown t-shirt slicked tight to his back as he walked through the shop, his scrutinizing gaze darted over the various trucks and construction equipment his boys were working on. Logan caught up with the Yeoman calling his name, a box sat cradled under her arm.

"What the fuck is this? I ain't expecting any packages." Logan growled, taking the box from the young girl's outstretched arm. No one ever sent him anything when he was deployed much less when he was in homeport; everyone in his family was either dead or estranged. Even his older brother Butch was still in jail in North Carolina for a drunk and disorderly last Logan knew, hell anything to do with Butch was usually bad news.

"Well, someone sent you a box Chief. You might as well open it and see what it is, might be cookies or something you can share with the shop." The Yeoman smiled brightly before turning on her heel, strutting away with a swing in her hips. Logan wiped his hand over his face; that girl could get herself into serious trouble with a swing like that, especially being where they were. She was too young for Logan-- being straight out of boot camp pretty much, and a relationship like that was severely frowned upon. Not that he was remotely interested in someone like YNSN Simmons, she was way too young and looked like the type who sought out trouble. Logan gave her a wide berth anytime she was near if he was able to.

Glancing at his watch, Logan realized if he was going to eat he needed to head off to the galley before it closed for the lunch clean up. Tucking the box under his arm, Logan handed off the leadership to his First Class Petty Officer who was changing the air filter on a deuce and a half. Logan barked at the tight bun of red hair that peeked out under the hood of the truck, muscles in her back and arms turning the wrench in her capable hands deftly.

"Heiderschiedt, I'm heading over to get some chow, you good to handle running the shop for a bit?" Logan's deep blue stare met with the clear green eyes of CM1 Melanie Heiderschiedt, they went pretty far back. Melanie was on her fourth deployment with Logan as her boss, making this Logan's sixth deployment in the twelve years he'd been in the Navy. Mels worked hard and played hard; she and Logan had thrown back more than a few beers over the years, not to mention throwing some punches together when the time called for it. They were co-workers and close friends, Logan knew he could count on Mels to run the shop in his absence.

Mels' lips twisted up into a tight grin, "Fuck you Dixon, you know I got it. Your skinny ass needs to eat so you get tubby like all the other Chiefs who walk around drinking coffee and never getting dirty. You're not like the rest of the Goat Locker, you never have been. What's that under your arm? Nobody ever sends you shit when we're gone." Mels yanked the box out from under Logan's arm, reading the flowery feminine return address.

"Ann Stranahan, Elmsford, NY. Well boss, looks like you got a female admirer, 'bout fucking time!" Mels' laughter caught Logan off guard as he snatched the box back from her, feeling the flush of embarrassment warming his ears.

"Fuck ya H-12, probably just some kid looking for pen pal and pattin' my back. Make sure #1710 gets out on the convoy tonight will ya?" Logan tucked the box back under his arm, turning to head out of the sweltering heat of the metal shop.

"Already did that or did you forget about Apra Harbor Dixon?" Mels' voice called after Logan, who flipped her the bird in response to Mels' throaty laughter.

Logan donned the Oakley's that were hiding in the thigh pocket of his BDU's. The Navy issued them to him, so why not wear them when the sun in the desert was bright as the flames of hell? Logan shook his head thinking about the temperature swings that were the norm for Iraq. 120 during the day and 80 or less at night, it felt like you were freezing when anywhere else it could be considered a warm night.

Logan stepped into the relative cool of the galley, seeing some of his mechanics eating over at a table in the corner. Passing through the line with his tray, Logan's face scrunched up at what was getting tossed on his tray. He wasn't quite sure if it was supposed to be fettuccini Alfredo or mac and cheese or if the pool of brown gravy was really gravy or beans of some sort. He never knew what anything was anymore when it came to meals, and at this half way point in the deployment it was better just to eat it than not.

Logan set his tray down at the table his men were eating at, setting the box off to the side. Unlike the other Chiefs who ate in the exclusive Goat Locker, he usually ate alone or with his mechanics. Logan didn't feel like he belonged with the college educated pretty boys or with the good ole boys, he felt most comfortable with the guys who got dirty for a living.

"Hey Chief, what's the box? You never get anything in the mail." CM2 Johnson flipped the box around to read the return address. It was postmarked almost a week ago from New York; a week was quick when it came to the mail finding them in the sands of Iraq. Everyone seemed to be curious as to what was in the box that bore Logan's name.

"Dunno. Simmons handed it off to me a bit ago." Logan grumbled around a mouthful of the mystery pasta in his mouth. He really didn't want to have to go through this with everyone in his work center, it was starting to get on his nerves and even his curiosity was starting to get the best of him as to the contents of the box.

"I'll bet its perfumed panties, a Hustler, cookies and a love note." CM3 Davidson piped up from the bottom end of the table, eliciting roars of laughter around the table.

"Nah, its perfumed panties, a naughty DVD and divorce papers." CMCN Reynolds poked next to Logan, which then got the shit eye from Logan.

"Watch it fucker. I'm not married. Never been. Keep it up smartass and I'll have you burning the latrines later." Logan snarled while pulling his knife out of his pocket, the flick of the blade opening quieting down the peanut gallery. Making short work of the tape seals on the box, he reached in to pull out six small bags of chocolate chip cookies, quickly pocketing two and tossing the rest on the table for the guys. Inside was a letter with his name and address on the receiver side and Ann's on the back of the envelope. Logan pocketed the letter; watching his guys mow through the four bags on the table, thanking him with mouths full of chocolate. He knew some of these guys didn't get boxes from home either, and it never hurt morale to share what little he had.

Nodding in his usual fashion; Logan dropped his tray off in the scrub side, dreading going back out into the heat of the day. He needed to check in with Mels and check off for the day. His work day was just about over anyway, it was time for CMC Stephens to get off his fat ass and get dirty. Logan didn't like the guy much, he never got dirty and always handed his work off to his minions. That wasn't how Logan thought a leader should be, and it wasn't how he worked if he could avoid it.

Logan found Mels changing the oil on #1710. Leave it to Mels to get the work done herself. She was a leader, she had Chief potential for sure. But the powers that be in upper command were hesitant to make a woman a CMC, in a mostly male work environment. Mels always had Logan's vote when it came time for her turn to get her anchor. Logan squatted down next to the feet sticking out from under the truck; tossing a bag of cookies on Mels crotch, making the woman startle and drop the drain plug in her hand.

"You think that much of me that you toss cookies in my crotch? Didn't know you cared Dixon." Mels' dirty face rolled out from under the truck, her teeth pearly white in the grime coating her features. Sitting up on the creeper Mels dug into the bag of cookies, her eyes closing in gratitude at the chocolate on her palate.

"Damn H-12, if I didn't know any better, I'd say ya just got off on that cookie." Logan grinned as Mels eyes popped open.

"Maybe I did, you know how women love chocolate better than sex. So what else was in the box?" Mels cocked an eyebrow at Logan, her curiosity piquing.

"Just a letter, figured I'd skate out of here and let Stephens waddle around sipping his coffee. All I need ya to do is have this one ready to go to the wire tonight. See you at muster tomorrow?" Logan always felt better after going back and forth with Mels, she was just one of the boys as far as he was concerned.

"Yeah. Get you some rest, you've been pushing it hard lately. I'll have this one out by the fence later tonight. Shouldn't take me but another hour to button it up. Thanks for the cookies, did you save any for yourself?" Mels made a habit of looking out for Logan, he was kind of like an older brother to her when it came down to it.

Logan patted his thigh pocket carefully, "Sure did. And you're welcome. See ya" Mels bumped fists with Logan before slinging back under the truck. Logan signed out of the computer, running his fingers through his short cropped hair before putting on his cover to leave the shop. Oakley's on, cover on, instant asshole. That was how many of the people in the battalion saw Logan, only the ones he let close knew he was so much more than that. Keeping up the tough but fair persona had gotten him far in the Navy, eight more years and he would be looking at retirement. Retired at 40 really didn't sound that bad, he would still be young enough to get a job wrenching and draw a paycheck plus retirement.

Walking across the compound, Logan returned the salutes of the officers and lower enlisted men he passed while making his way to his conex box. Logan unlocked his personal quarters that really were quite a bit smaller than his bedroom at the house in Colorado he shared with Mels. Double bed against the wall with a locker underneath it, desk with a laptop against the other wall, a just barely big enough stall shower and a locker was the extent of the furnishings in the small space. Unloading his pockets onto the desk, Logan's eyes flitted over the white envelope with Ann Stranahan's address on it. Logan groaned when the AC kicked on, the blast of cold air felt amazing on his tanned sweaty skin. Stripping off the sweat soaked t-shirt; and unbuttoning his pants made Logan feel about ten times cooler sitting half naked at his desk, turning the letter from Ann over in his hands.

He really didn't get why this girl would send him cookies, it wasn't like he knew her, knowing for a fact none of his guys had the last name of Stranahan. Mentally going through the short list of girlfriends he had in his life, none of them had the last name of Stranahan either. Curiosity ate at him; Logan ran the blade of his knife through the seam of the envelope. The delicate scent of a floral perfume invaded the space, momentarily masking the smells of Iraq. His eyes read over the neatly handwritten letter, the text answering most of the questions as to why Ann would be sending him cookies and who she was. Leaving the letter open on his desk, Logan divested of his pants and boots. The shower sounded like a great idea before he hit the sack, tomorrow was another early day working in hell for the world's greatest Navy.

Chapter Three

Ann ran out to her truck from the hospital's employee entrance, it was hard to breathe with the frigid air biting at her lungs. She was shadowing Dr. Helton today for class, studying the effects of psychotropic drugs via MRI to help heal brain injuries. It hadn't gone smoothly; the veteran warned the staff beforehand that he needed something for his claustrophobia and anxiety. When the man threw the nurse against the wall in his fearful state, Ann was more than glad she was standing on the other side of the glass wall. It broke her heart seeing how these once strong, proud and whole men and women came back from war broken by what they experienced. Instead of reading about it or hearing about it on the news, she now saw with her own eyes a glimpse into the horrors they lived with every day.

Ann reached into her mailbox, pulling out the stack of mail that had been forgotten over the week. Flipping through the envelopes with school letter head on the corner, the electric bill and her credit card bill, she just about dropped the whole pile when she came upon the last envelope.

The dirty envelope was a bit banged up, but the blocky script in the upper left corner explained why the poor thing was a little worse for wear. The return address was Camp Fallujah, Iraq-- Logan had taken time out of his day to write her. The postmark was almost two weeks before, which meant Logan had probably wrote it shortly after getting her care package. Ann was more than shocked, putting the letter on top of the pile as she walked up to her apartment, her heart beating fast in her chest.

Ann hung up her jacket while toeing out of her boots, proceeding to flop down onto the sofa beside the picture window. Tossing all the other mail onto the coffee table, she carefully opened the letter from Logan, her eyes glued to his blocky handwriting.

Dear Ann,

I've never got a box in the mail from anyone when I've been deployed, so your box was a total surprise. Thanks for the cookies; me and my guys loved them. I'm doing pretty alright considering where I'm at. Can't give you exact details of what I do, mail sometimes gets screened for passing of sensitive info. I ain't got family to miss me over here, so I guess that makes it easier.

I can tell you that I'm a Seabee mechanic in the Navy. I work on trucks, buses, and construction equipment. Sometimes the nationals bring in stuff and we work on that too. I help keep the guys going that build shit over here, like roads, schools and bridges. The Seabee motto kinda tells it all: "We Build, We Fight."

My days are really hot, fuck it feels like hell on Earth. Especially when it hits 120 during the day. I get up early, go to *muster and get my people going on the fix it list. I eat lunch, work some more, eat dinner, and have a little bit of free time to myself. I'm using that free time to write you back, although I ain't sure why. Usually I spend it playing cards or rugby with friends.*

Yeah I like what I do for the most part, pays better than the jobs back in the states. The only bad part is the bad guys out there on the other side of the wire that are trying to kill us. What you see on the news ain't what happens over here, trust me when I say that. This ain't a great place to be, armpit of the world.

Gotta get going, morning comes too fucking early. Thanks again for the cookies; a lot of my guys over here sure appreciated them.

Respectfully,

CMC Dixon

Ann was surprised at the half page sitting in her hands, she didn't expect the guy to write back to be honest. It sounded like he was really busy over there with his work, and that where he was wasn't the safest place to be. The idea of anything over 90 degrees made Ann think about sweating her brains out. There were plenty of times when she was home in Georgia that the summers got up to 100, and she begged her father to get A/C put in. But her pleas fell on deaf ears, the farmhouse was a hundred plus years old. A/C just wasn't possible.

Ann carefully set Logan's letter aside, going through the rest of the mail. In a week she would be leaving for Christmas break to go home to the farm in Georgia. While she was glad to be going home to her family, her heart was heavy thinking about Logan halfway across the world not having a family to come home to for Christmas, much less having someone send him a Christmas package. It was then that Ann decided to make it her mission to put together a Christmas care package for Logan. She hoped he would appreciate getting the care package and what she had planned to go inside it.

Ann roamed through the aisles at Target, grabbing a copy of the book Leah had loaned her, along with a handful of her favorite cd's. She snatched up a few bags of Christmas candy, a Christmas card and a few of the travel size bathroom items she had recalled a website saying service members deployed always appreciated. Ann pulled out the gift card that Aunt Patricia and Uncle Otis sent her for Christmas, thinking the money was better spent on Logan than Ann just blowing it on clothes.

After getting home, Ann sat down with her notebook and pen once again to reply to Logan's letter. This letter came out quite a bit longer than her initial letter; it was her hope he would continue writing her, just so he had someone to write home to. She carefully folded up the letter, tucking it into the card and putting it in with everything else. Ann had bought so much stuff that it was a challenge getting it to all fit in the box the postmaster gave her the last time she was in the post office. Apparently there were special boxes for sending off care packages to deployed troops that got special rates. The postmaster had also let Ann know that boxes "usually" took two weeks to get to the final destination, but that it could sometimes take longer with holidays and the movement of the mail through the combat zones. Ann hoped this box would get to Logan before Christmas, but with Christmas being less than two weeks away she didn't put much faith in it.

A text message pinged on Ann's phone as she set the care package by the door to go out in the morning mail. It was almost dinner time, so it could be any one of her friends or her sister Krista. Krista had yet to check in for the day; Ann was beginning to miss their little routine of joking back and forth. Picking up the phone, Ann shrugged at the message from Leah.

Haven't seen u in 2 wks. U ok?

Between classes, studying, work and shadowing Ann didn't have time to do much of anything she wanted to do. Leah, being her best friend, was not only concerned but also nosey as all get out. Ann decided it was best to answer before a flood of messages came through and made her phone hiccup.

Been busy with class, work, studying. Something you should do every so often. I'm fine. What's up?

Feel like going out? Dinner/beers on me

Ann sighed, it would be the last time she would get to see Leah before heading home for Christmas break, beers and dinner didn't sound like a bad idea.

What about Applebee's in Tarrytown? We haven't been there in a while?

Sounds good Ann, get your lazy ass ready, omw!

Leah lived 20 minutes away in Valhalla, which meant there was no reason for Ann to even try and do her hair or make up. Pulling on a hoodie and ball cap, Ann ran her fingertips over the box sitting on the arm of the sofa. She had to remember to take that box to the post office in the morning and hope it got to Logan before Christmas.

Leah opened the door to Ann's apartment, almost hitting Ann with the door.

"Shit Ann! Sorry, didn't think you'd be standing there waiting on me! I guess you're ready to go?" Leah couldn't hide the embarrassment on her face of almost nailing her best friend with the door.

"It's ok; I should have been paying more attention. Yeah, I'm ready to go. Do you remember what time the post office in Tarrytown closes? I kinda want to get this box out tonight." Ann couldn't remember when the post office closed, but she knew it was later with it being the holiday season.

Leah picked up the box; her gaze falling on the recipient's address, reading it aloud to herself trying to make sense of it.

"I think they close at 6, I think we can make it just in time. Why are you sending a box off to some guy in Iraq? Do you have a boyfriend I don't know about?" Leah picked at Ann who blushed pink in the cheeks.

"Come on, let's go. I'll explain on the way to the post office. I want to try and get this to him before Christmas." Ann muttered, snatching the box from Leah and ushering her out the door.

Leah darted her BMW through traffic like she was on a mission from God. Keeping her eyes trained on the road, she started off with the obvious question that was hanging in the air like a wet towel.

"So why the box to a guy in Iraq? I know you Ann, if you had a boyfriend you would tell me. Sooo….who's the guy?" Leah maneuvered around a slow moving commuter bus as if it wasn't moving at all.

Ann took a deep breath, her eyes settling on the box in her lap, her thoughts going back to the letter that was sitting on her kitchen bar.

"He's a deployed Seabee with the Navy in Iraq. His name is Logan Dixon, and he's a mechanic. I got his name from the Holidays for Heroes tree at church, which you wouldn't know about since you're usually hung over on Sunday. I sent him a box of cookies a couple of weeks ago and he sent me a letter back thanking me for the cookies. He said no one ever sends him things when he is deployed because he doesn't have a family, and I thought that I would send him a Christmas box. No one should go without having something for Christmas you know? And as far as a boyfriend, *if* I had one I would totally tell you Leah. I promise."

Leah nodded, "Well I'd expect you to tell me about a boyfriend and it's nice of you to send the guy boxes of stuff. Geeze I feel bad for him being over there in Iraq, shit's really hitting the fan around Fallujah and the Anbar Providence. Feel even worse that he doesn't have anyone back here either, at least he's got you Ann. You're so sweet ya know?" Leah grinned, pinching Ann's thigh through her form fitting jeans.

"Ow! Jesus Leah! How do you know about Fallujah and the Anbar Providence? You never do anything but party and seldom do you ever go to class!" Ann threw the truth out there as much as it may have hurt Leah's feelings; it was a wonder how she was making through medical school.

Leah scoffed, pulling into a parking spot at the post office. "Oh honey, there is this cute officer recruiter for the Navy, trying to recruit the med students at school in the commons. I've been nosing around him asking questions and listening to him talk. Go on and get your ass in

there so that box can get on its way!"
Leah unlocked the door of the car,
effectively kicking Ann out.

It never shocked Ann when Leah
was out on the prowl and how she went
about hooking up. It seemed like she had
a different man in her bed every week, but
yet was clean as sterile cotton.

Standing in the line at the post
office, Ann watched people mailing off
boxes of various sizes and shapes to
locations all over the world. When it
became her time to pass off her box and
pay, the elderly post master smiled at Ann
with a grin that lit up the room. Ann
noticed the name tag on his shirt read
"Tom", she had never noticed it the last
time she had brought that first box in to
mail off.

"Another box to Iraq huh? I'm sure
this fella is sure appreciating you sending
love from home. He's a lucky Seabee to be
with a gal like you. The missus sent me
packages when I was gone during the war

too. I'm sure half of what she sent ended up somewhere else and I got what was left. $23.46 sweetheart."

Ann slid her debit card, her eyes catching the faded Seabee tattoo on Tom's forearm. "You were a Seabee during WWII?"

"Sure was sweetie. I served under the King Bee himself Ben Moreell; we built roads and runways in Japan. Helped turn the tide during the war. Next time you write your 'Bee tell him I said Can Do. He'll understand. I'll make sure this goes out in tonight's mail personally," Tom winked at Ann, making her grin, blush and giggle. "It should be there by Christmas. Chief Dixon will be glad to see it. You have yourself a Merry Christmas Miss Stranahan."

Ann smiled, "Thank you Sir. You have a Merry Christmas as well and thank you for your service." Ann darted out of the post office, feeling giddy that the postmaster was friendly with her and aware of how important it was to her that the box went out in the night's mail. She would have to make sure to hand her boxes off to Tom the next time she was in the post office.

The cheesy grin plastered on Ann's face made Leah smile, "Everything go ok? Get it out tonight? You look like the cat that just ate the mouse!"

"Let's just say I have an elf on my side for this box to make it to Iraq for Christmas. Hey aren't we going out to eat?" Ann poked Leah in the ribs, "You were the one who said you were paying for beers and dinner."

Leah couldn't help but laugh, "Oh Ann, you never let me forget when I'm paying. Come on let's go feed you; you're way too skinny these days. You need to put some weight on so your Seabee boyfriend doesn't break you when he comes home!"

Ann feigned shock, breaking out in hearty laughs with Leah. She was right, Ann did need a night out with her best friend. But she couldn't keep her thoughts on the backside off of Logan in Iraq, working and in danger. Ann whispered a silent prayer for his safety, hoping that someone upstairs was listening and sending an angel to watch over him.

Chapter Four

Logan was in a foul mood, Stephens had left two trucks out unserviceable because he was too lazy to get his fat ass moving on them. Logan was the one who got his ass tore by the higher ups, the trucks were needed out on a project in the morning. Logan had grabbed Mels along with Johnson, working through most of the night to get the trucks going. Johnson had stepped out to bring back food from the galley, as Logan and Mels finished up the last truck. Logan was wiping his hands clean, guiding Mels out of the shop to get the truck into the yard. Logan sent Mels to bed, finishing up the log for the next crew to take over. The shop ran 24/7 on deployment, but Logan felt the one responsible for making things runs smoothly. It was his job being in the leadership role of Chief; sometimes he took that job a bit too seriously.

Logan was surprised when he heard the shower running in his quarters. Only one other person knew the combination to his lock, and that person was standing in his shower sluicing water off her very naked and curvy body. What Mels looked like in uniform was much different than what Mels looked like naked. The uniform hid the curves that made her definitely woman, curves Logan knew intimately. At one point, when they were both CM1, Logan and Mels had been something. Not really a couple in the usual sense of the word, but something like very close friends that made weekends pass in bed together. Now, with Logan being her Chief and Mels still a CM1, all they could be were friends in the Navy's eyes. But back home in Colorado they shared a house, each with their own bedrooms. They never got back to being in bed together after Apra Harbor. Logan never knew what happened, but after they got back from Guam, he wasn't welcome in Mels' bed anymore.

Logan stripped down to just his BDU pants, sitting at his open laptop on the desk. Logging into Navy Federal online, he paid the house payment, his truck and his motorcycle before they were due. Next paycheck he would cover the payment to the neighbor boarding his horses, the utilities and the maid that came in to clean and check on the house while they were gone. Logan jumped; feeling Mels' fingers digging into his shoulders, attempting to work out the knots. He hadn't even been aware of the shower shutting off less than eight feet away from him.

"You're tense Logan. You need to relax before you break something." Mels whispered in his ear, knowing her calling him by his first name would elicit an interesting response from him. Outside the door of his quarters it was last names only, professional all the way. Inside his quarters it was personal, first names and close. Mels lived out in the women's barracks, sharing a dorm room with four other First Class Petty Officer females. She didn't have the luxury of a private room with shower like Logan did. Being a Chief had its perks, along with the responsibility.

Logan turned around in the chair, a shit eating grin plastered on his face. Mels cocked her head and licked her lips seductively, knowing full well what was running through Logan's head. She knew exactly how long it had been since he last got laid, since what's-her-name with the black hair and tattoos dumped him right before they left on deployment. That was a mistake that Mels knew was going to blow up in his face; after one look at the rock and roll queenie, Mels knew she was all wrong for country boy Logan.

"Mels, ya know damn well you kicked me out of ya bed back after Apra Harbor. And we ain't been back since. I don't plan on that changing either, even with ya standing in my quarters naked and wet." Logan left the innuendo hanging in the air between them, Mels was smart enough to figure it out.

Logan stood up, closing the distance between his and Mels' chest. He could almost swear he smelled her; she was that hot for him. Mels swallowed hard; she could feel her skin vibrating this close to Logan's skin, memories of Apra Harbor flooding her brain.

"Come on Logan, you got to admit that you're getting awfully tired of your hand at this point in the deployment. I've got an ache and you've got needs. Whaddya say for old time's sake?" Mels ran her short nails over Logan's chest, his eyes dropping to her full bare breasts. She could tell he was considering it, his breathing had changed just enough for her to notice as well as she knew him.

"Mels, as much as I wouldn't mind throwing ya down on the bed and fucking you six ways to Sunday, it ain't gonna happen. I barely have time to take a shit much less jack off, so sex is the last thought on my mind. I ain't gonna chance knockin' you up so you get sent home either; I need you here turnin' wrenches. Ain't gonna lie, after you kicked me out of ya bed after Apra Harbor, I'm still hurt. I love ya honey, but we ain't like that no more. So why don't you just get dressed and head off to bed before you do something we'll both regret? I'll see you at muster in the morning." Logan laid his knuckles against Mels' cheek, seeing the sting of rejection taking hold. He knew it would hurt her; him turning her down, but she never knew how much it hurt him when she kicked him out of her bed.

Mels huffed, turning to the bed to get dressed in her pt gear. Logan watched as she pulled the shorts over her hips, the t-shirt over her head. Mels angrily tied on her sneakers, pulling the laces more than tight. He could tell she was mad, but she wouldn't stay mad for long. Even when she was raging pissed at him, Mels always came back and he didn't know why. Underneath Mels clothes was a white box, Logan glanced at the addressee side, seeing it was for him.

Mels handed the box to Logan, her eyes downcast on the addresses. "Oh by the way, Simmons gave this to me tonight to give to you. That was why I was originally here. Merry Christmas Dixon." Mels gathered up her dirty clothes, closing the door to Logan's quarters behind her. Logan stood there with a dumb look on his face, was it really Christmas? Not that days really had any meaning on a deployment until you hit the last two weeks, but how could he miss Christmas? Logan sat back down at his laptop; looking down in the corner of the screen, it read 1:30am 12/25/2008. It had just turned Christmas day in Colorado, indeed it was Christmas.

Logan turned the box around to face him, seeing Ann's address in New York in the upper left corner again. This box was bigger than the last one, heavier as well. Taking out his knife, Logan split the tape holding the box together. The box popped open with the pressure of the tape relieved. On top was a green envelope; Logan set the rest of the box aside, his knife running under the flap of the envelope. Logan opened the card, a letter fell into his lap.

Ann had signed the card:

"Merry Christmas Logan- Ann."

He caught himself smiling at the fact that Ann thought enough of him to send him a Christmas box. Something about this girl was different, she didn't know him from Adam's housecat but yet she took time out of her day to think of him. That had to count for something.

Opening the letter, Logan still caught the faint scent of delicate floral perfume on the pages. The scent stirred thoughts of Colorado summer time in a clearing of flowers out in the mountains. Closing his eyes; Logan imagined Ann barefoot in a summer dress, all tanned skin and blonde hair standing in that clearing looking at him. He had no clue whatsoever what she looked like, but the scent made him think of a blonde. Not that it mattered to him really what she looked like; she was in New York, he was in Iraq. Nothing would come of it; other than maybe friends that he was sure of.

Dear Logan,

Hi, how are you? I hope this box finds you before Christmas, and doing as well as you can be where you are. I'm glad you and your guys liked the cookies I sent in my last box; sorry I didn't send any this time. I thought with it being Christmas and all you wouldn't mind some Christmas candy. I'll send cookies in my next box if you'd like, just let me know ok?

Thanks for clearing things up a little bit about what you do for work and what you do over there. I can't imagine someone wanting to kill you one day and then asking for your help the next, it just doesn't make sense. But I guess that's life at war right?

120 during the day? Is that a normal occurrence? I begged my Dad to put A/C in our farmhouse the one summer it hit 100 for a week. He told me no, that the house is too old. I have A/C in my apartment here in New York though; it's nice in the summer. Gosh, I hope you have some way of cooling off over there. I'd be worried about heat exhaustion if I were you!

Your day's sound pretty full and busy, thank you so much for taking a minute out of it to write me back, I really appreciate it! I can't play cards, I suck at bluffing. I've never heard of rugby, I guess I'll see if I can find some matches online to watch so I can have an idea of what it is.

Well, I guess since you shared a little bit about you, I should share a little bit about me. I'm from a farm in Georgia, but I go to medical school in New York State. I just started my sixth year this fall, so I have a whole 'nother full year ahead of me. Once I graduate I can apply for my licensure in any state and practice as a doctor. I've still got to figure out what I want to specialize in; I have a couple of ideas but nothing concrete. I like helping people, so I guess being a doctor is a good way of doing that.

I'm still a farm girl in the city, my classmates like to poke fun at me sometimes when I talk. I guess my accent is still there, even though I don't realize it unless my parents call and I talk to them. I have an older sister named Krista, she works as my dad's veterinary assistant on the farm. My dad's the local vet, my mom used to teach school until she retired from that. I go to church every Sunday, hang out with my friends when I can. But I think I spend most of my time at school, working or studying. I guess I'm kind of like you, pretty busy.

I've seen that the fighting is getting pretty bad where you are; I pray for you every night that you're safe over there. I guess since you have no one over here to worry about you, I will. I hope that doesn't make you feel weird or anything.

So where are you from originally? Do you (or did you have any) siblings? What kind of things do you like? I put some of my favorite cd's in this box, I hope you like them. I really didn't know what to put in this box, so I wandered around Target and let things come to me. You're the first person I've ever sent anything to who was deployed, would you let me know if there is something you'd like? I'll try and get it into the next box, if you'd like.

I hope you have a Merry Christmas. I'll be at my parent's house until mid-January, so if you'd like to write me back there that would be nice. If you think that your reply won't get to me until after January 10th, then please send it to my address in New York.

Take Care,

Ann

Logan took note of the address in Hazlehurst, Georgia underneath Ann's signature. Having no idea where that was, Logan pulled it up on Google Maps. In the starting point field he plugged in his hometown of Clayton, GA and Hazlehurst into the destination field. Looking at the mapped out results, Logan realized Ann was from far South Georgia compared to him. It would take almost five hours to get to her hometown from his, not that it mattered anymore. Curiosity getting the better of him, he plugged in her address in Elmsford, NY, leaving Hazlehurst as the destination. He hoped she wasn't driving home for Christmas that was a 14 hour drive.

A drive like that was nothing for Logan; he'd driven from Colorado to Georgia once. That was a long drive to bury his Grandpa, Butch didn't even show up for it. The least the son of a bitch could have done was show up for the man that pretty much raised him and Logan after their Dad decided to live at the bar.

Logan dug through the box, pulling out a book, five cd's, a gallon Ziploc bag full of bathroom stuff and four bags of Christmas candy. He'd keep the bathroom stuff, but the candy would find a home in the shop. Logan wasn't big on candy, but cookies, cake and pie were fair game. Flipping through the cd's, he was surprised by the diversity of the genres. Nickelback, George Strait, Songs of Ireland, Staind and Andrea Bocelli. He knew three of the five, the music from Ireland he had an idea about, but the last cd piqued his curiosity.

Putting the disc in his laptop, Logan was surprised by the voice of the opera tenor that filled the small space of his quarters. The music was hauntingly soothing to him, it wasn't like anything he had ever heard before. Turning the volume down to where he could barely hear it, Logan took a quick shower before crawling into bed. The operatic notes lulling him into a deep, dreamless sleep.

Chapter Five

A shadow fell over the book Ann was curled up reading in the picture window of her bedroom. Since she was a small girl, the picture window had been her favorite place to read. She could look out over the pastures of the farm and see everything that she knew and loved, this was her sanctuary from the busy life she led in New York. It was as if she literally was two people inside one- Ann the farm girl and Ann the city girl. Ann looked up from the text on the effects of traumatic brain injuries on the psychological state to see Krista grinning at her.

"Hey bookworm, what're ya reading about?" Krista poked at her younger sister, plopping down next to her in the picture window, happily munching on an apple.

Ann stuck her bookmark in the page, gently closing the book. "The effects of traumatic brain injuries on personality. There was a veteran in the hospital being treated for his TBI and I witnessed what happened when they tried to put him in a MRI, it wasn't pretty. I feel so bad for the military members coming home and their injuries from war. I was thinking of maybe specializing in neurology, something to try and help. What are you doing?"

Ann snatched the apple out of her older sister's hand, taking a large bite out of the Granny Smith. Krista feigned shock, smiling brightly. "You know, rather than being stuck in your books you should eat and get out more. I was thinking since it's your last night in town we could go up to Hank's and have some beers and dinner. Mine and Ryan's treat."

Krista had been dating Ryan for almost a year now. They had met when Krista tried a year at college up in Athens, when that didn't work out Ryan moved to Hazlehurst for Krista. Ann couldn't imagine leaving everything and everyone she knew and loved behind for someone. She did it for college, but she planned on coming back once she graduated. Ann didn't know how Ryan did it, probably because he was welcomed into the Stranahan family with open arms.

Ann sighed, handing the apple back to Krista before she took another bite. "You're right you know. I need to get out more, and food doesn't sound bad." Ann's stomach growled stridently at that point, making the sisters laugh out loud.

"Come on Ann, I'll text Ryan and let him know we're leaving. We'll probably be out late, so make sure you bring a sweater." Krista tossed her arm over Ann's shoulder, pulling her sister into a hug. "Miss having you home kiddo. Can't wait till you graduate next year and come home. It'll be like old times, going out swimming in the pond and riding the horses."

Ann laughed at some of the memories flashing through her mind as they walked into the kitchen. Ann could smell her mother baking cookies, the chocolate making her mouth water. "Oh mom, your cookies always make me want to eat the entire tray!" She snatched a cookie off the cooling rack, closing her eyes at the ooey gooey goodness invading her mouth. No matter how bad her day was, Annette's cookies made everything better.

Annette chuckled at her youngest gushing over cookies, "You're welcome sweetheart. Hopefully your young man in Iraq enjoyed them as much as you do."

Krista gave her sister a questioning look, wondering what Annette was talking about. Ann waved her off, hoping to explain later. She didn't think it was such a big deal, but Krista being Krista would think everything and anything about it. Especially since as far as Krista knew, the last person Ann had dated was Dustin Rogers in high school. Krista gave Ann that look- the one Ann knew meant she was explaining something later.

"And just where are you two girls off to tonight?" Warren came through the kitchen from the mud room, drying his hands on a towel. He was glad to have his daughters home with him, but sad to see Ann leaving in the morning to go back to school in New York.

"Krista and Ryan are taking me out to Hank's for dinner before I go." Ann skipped over to her father, wrapping her arms around his barrel chest and hugging him. She had always been Warren's favorite, probably because she was the youngest and the best surprise he and Annette ever had. He was sad to see her leaving in the morning, but knew her time in New York was coming to a close.

"That sounds like a good time. You girls have fun and stay out of trouble." Warren's soft voice carried through the kitchen, making Annette hide a smile behind her hand. Even though his daughters were grown women now, the fatherly instinct wouldn't leave him.

"Oh we will Daddy. See you later!" Krista called over her shoulder, tugging

Ann along by the hand, giggling like little girls.

Ann sat down in the booth across from Krista and Ryan, who both had beers sitting in front of them. Ann was still waiting on her Jameson and Coke, she really didn't feel like beer tonight.

"So what's this Annette was saying you have a guy in Iraq that she's sending cookies to?" Krista took long gulp out of the beer, eyeing Ann over the glass.

"Mom's not sending him cookies, I made him her cookies and sent them a few weeks ago. I sent him a Christmas box before I left New York. I haven't heard back from him yet, so I hope he got the box and is okay." Ann reached for the glass the waitress set in front of her, the whiskey warming her throat on the way down.

"Iraq's a hotbed of fighting right now Ann. Hopefully he's okay. Does he have a name? What does he do?" Ryan was the one who kept up on current events, he had a brother who was in the Army stationed in Ft. Benning. Dan was still in the states as far as Ryan knew, but with him being a Paratrooper he could leave at any time for anywhere.

Ann related all the information she knew about Logan to her sister and boyfriend, drinking through the Jameson and Coke a bit quicker than she realized.

"Have you ever seen this guy? Like pictures? Do you even know how old he is? For all you know he could be Daddy's age!" Krista joked, causing Ryan to snicker and Ann to choke on her drink.

"I've never asked him his age, and I haven't seen a picture either. We aren't like dating or anything. He's just a guy who has no family that I thought I would be nice to. I guess you could say we're kinda sorta friends?" Ann sighed when the waitress brought her another drink, tonight was a night to enjoy out with family and friends.

Krista's eyes popped open wide, nearly dropping her fork at the sight of the mountain of a man who stopped by their table. It had been years since she had seen him last, and he had definitely grown out and up. Ann turned her head following Krista's line of vision; her gaze fell on a bronc riding belt buckle holding a tight pair of jeans together. She felt the blush rise on her face, being so up close and personal to whoever the man was.

"Hey Ann, hey Krista, haven't seen you guys in a long time. How ya been?" Ann knew that voice like she knew what day of the week it was. Dustin Rogers had been her boyfriend all through high school. His family moved out west for him to attend college in Montana after high school, and the long distance relationship had fizzled out over time.

"I'm good. This is my boyfriend Ryan Kennedy. Ryan, this is Dustin Rogers. He's a friend of the family." Krista beamed, as Ryan reached out to shake the large hand Dustin offered.

"Nice to meet you Dustin." Ryan grinned, clearly feeling good after a few beers.

Dustin nodded, looking down at Ann, "Mind if I sit with y'all a bit?" Ann swallowed and nodded slowly. She couldn't take her eyes off how Dustin had changed since she last saw him. He was taller, filled out, rugged and he smelled good. Dustin smiled sliding into the booth next to Ann, ordering a beer when the waitress came by to check on them.

"How ya been Ann? You look great!" Dustin flashed a bright white smile, making Ann stare.

"Um, I'm good. You look pretty good yourself. Looks like Montana's been good to you. Did you finish college yet?" Ann stammered, taking a large bite of her whiskey chicken to hide her embarrassment.

"Yeah, I graduated from U of M two years ago with a Bachelor's in Rangeland

Ecology and Watershed Management. I work for the Fish and Wildlife as a Game Warden. I love it out there, it's so much different than it is here. You should come out and visit sometime. I've got a cabin up near the Kootenai National Forest, beautiful views of the mountains." Dustin glanced over at Ann as he talked, making eye contact a few times.

"That's great that you graduated and you have a job you love, way to go! It sounds like you're really enjoying your life out west. Ann is still in college, but she graduates next year. Tell him Ann!" If looks could have killed, Krista would have been dead with Ann eyeing her down.

Ann set her fork down, wiping her mouth with a napkin, turning to look at Dustin. Swallowing the knot in her throat, Ann told Dustin about how she was still in medical school in New York and that she was proud of him for finishing college and getting a job he loved. The guy grinned the entire time Ann talked, if he could have eaten her words with a fork, she was sure he would have wolfed them down.

"So what are you doing back here from Montana then?" Ann picked up her fork, continuing to eat after talking about herself. Things didn't seem so awkward sitting next to Dustin and eating dinner, it was as if distance had never come between them.

"We always come back around Christmas to see the family. Dad's doing really well out there in the energy boom, so we have the time and money to come back. You should come out sometime Ann." Dustin ran his fingers along Ann's thigh under the table, making her choke on her drink.

Ann could tell from the look on Krista's face that she was caught like a deer in the headlights. Not that she was uncomfortable, it was just different to have someone be interested in her. None of her friends or classmates in New York showed any interest in her, so Dustin showing interest made butterflies in Ann's stomach.

"I'll think about it. Maybe I can come out for a bit over summer break? Is that a good time for sightseeing in Montana?" Ann wouldn't mind seeing the mountains, get a break away from Georgia and New York.

"Sure, summer is a great time to see Montana. Let me know when and I'll pick you up at the airport. There's so much I can show you, it'll be a good time."

The waitress brought by the bill, which Dustin promptly took and paid. Krista opened her mouth to say something, Dustin waved her off saying it was the least he could do for old friends. Ann graciously thanked him, as they walked out to the parking lot. Dustin opened Ann's door for her, handing her a napkin with his number wrote on it.

"Give me a call sometime Ann, I'd love to see you again," he breathed next to her ear, kissing her cheek lightly.

Ann blushed, tucking the napkin into the visor of her Explorer. "I will. You take care Dustin. Thank you for dinner." Ann could hear Krista trying to stifle her giggles in the backseat.

Dustin leaned in the window, brushing his fingers over Ann's cheek. "You're welcome sweetheart. I had a good time, see you soon." Dustin leaned in just a bit farther, his lips brushing against Ann's. That was all it took for the electricity to run up Ann's spine, her breath catching in her throat. Dustin pulled away, a lopsided smirk on his face.

Ann watched him walk away in those tight Wrangler jeans, Krista almost howling with fits of laughter in the backseat.

"Oh shut up! Both of you!" Ann barked as she glared at them both in the rearview mirror, pulling out onto the county road and heading for the house Krista shared with Ryan. She was glad to be dropping those two off, Ann wasn't sure if she could handle any more of Krista's drunk laughter or giving Ann hell about Dustin.

Ann snagged Dustin's phone number out of the visor, adding it to her contacts before going upstairs to her room. She still had to pack, Ann was notorious for waiting until the very last minute to leave home. Mama and Daddy were already in bed for the night, Daddy had always been an early riser.

Ann sighed when she saw Annette had washed and folded all her clothes, leaving them in neat stacks on Ann's bed. A note accompanied the clothes, making her lips quirk up in a smile.

Honey,

Daddy and I are so glad to have you home, even if for a short while. We are so proud of you and wish you safe travels on your way back to school. Call when you get there.

Love,

Mom

Ps. Good luck with your young man in Iraq, I'm sure he's a keeper!

Ann groaned at the postscript, knowing that Annette didn't know any better. What was the point of correcting her? Who knew if anything would come of it later on when Logan got back to the States? Right now they were just acquaintances that exchanged letters, it could go anywhere as far as Ann could guess.

Ann sent Dustin a text with her number, he sent back a message of thanks, wishing her a goodnight and he would talk to her later. She plugged the phone in, setting out pajamas and clothes for tomorrow, packing the rest away. Changing into her pajamas; Ann stretched out in her bed, the cool sheets pulling her into a comfortable sleep.

Chapter Six

Ann pulled her Explorer right up to the wrap around front porch of the house, Daddy standing there holding her bags. Annette held a bag of cookies in her hand, knowing they would probably be long gone before her daughter got back to school. Warren popped the back tailgate, loading Ann's bags in the back, watching her step out of the truck to come tell her parents goodbye. Annette wrapped Ann in a tight hug, it wasn't easy for her to tell Ann goodbye, no matter if it was the first time or the last time. Annette always had problems with it, even with Ann being a grown woman.

"You stop for the night when you get tired. New York is a long drive. Call when you stop and call when you get there you hear?" Annette's order came firm through her tears.

Ann took the bag of cookies from her mother, grinning at the repeat performance of what happened at the end of summer break.

"I'll be fine mama. I'll call like always, I promise." Ann pushed up on her tip toes to kiss her mother's cheek, assuring her that Ann understood and heeded her words.

Warren pulled his youngest into his chest, hugging her tightly as he kissed the top of Ann's head. "You know this never gets any easier. I'll be glad when you are home for good. Drive safely. I know you will probably hit some snow up in Virginia or Maryland."

"I know Daddy. I love you too. Only another year after this semester and I'll be home, I promise." Ann let go of her father, walking back to her truck and sliding into the driver's seat.

Just as Ann put the truck in drive, she looked back in her side mirror to see Daddy running up to the side of the truck, something in his hand. Ann stopped;

rolling down her window to see what it was that he had.

"Ann, I'm sorry I forgot to give this to you this morning. It came in yesterday's mail for you." Warren took a deep breath, handing Ann the slightly thick beat up white envelope. Ann knew exactly what it was when she saw the blocky script on the addressee side. Logan had written a reply to her Christmas letter, and by luck it had arrived before she left home. Had it been a day later, Ann would have been gone. But Annette would have mailed the letter to New York, of that Ann was sure.

Ann took the envelope from her father, leaning out to kiss his cheek, "Thanks Daddy. I love you!" Ann couldn't hide the grin that lit up her delicate features.

Warren patted his daughter's face, "Be careful going back Ann. Call when you stop tonight."

Ann nodded, setting the envelope on the passenger seat next to her purse with care. She always hated making this drive back, part of her seemed to stay in Georgia where life was simpler. But when it came to picking a medical school that was affordable with a positive graduation rate, New York was the winning choice. All she had to keep telling herself was that it was only another year and she would be done. Ann called Leah, asking to see if she was back in town and would stop by Ann's apartment and check on things. What Ann had originally thought to be a few minutes of phone call, poured into two hours of gossip about home and upcoming classes.

The traffic wasn't too bad once she got north of Fayetteville, NC. She loved the look of the hills and mountains around her, it reminded her of the landscape in upstate New York. Ann couldn't wait to get home to her own bed, but she knew it was a two day drive, especially driving by herself. She always took two days driving down and back, unless she could talk Leah into going with her. Ann smirked at the memory of when city girl Leah went down to Georgia with her over summer; it was a hoot hearing Leah complain about the smells of the farm and the "huge ass" bugs. Ann didn't think her parents were too pleased with Leah's colorful vernacular; but by the time they left for the summer, Ann's parents had fallen in love with Leah and Leah had learned to appreciate the country life.

Rain plagued the interstate once Ann crossed the state line into Virginia at Roanoke Rapids, NC. After pushing through an hour and a half of steady rain Ann pulled into a hotel in Ashland, VA. She was soaking wet by the time she got her bag and purse into the spacious and cozy hotel room. Stripping off her wet clothes, Ann groaned when the hot water sprayed on her chilled skin. Brushing her wet hair out straight before tying it up in a loose ponytail, Ann remembered she needed to call her parents before they went to bed for the night.

She reached out to grab her purse off the desk, finding her cellphone nestled up against Logan's letter. Ann couldn't

remember when she put the letter in her
purse, it must have been during one of the
times she stopped for gas. She absently
dialed the number to her parent's house,
hearing it ring three times before her
father picked up. Warren was glad to hear
his daughter's voice, asking where she
was and reminding her it was dinner time.
Ann couldn't help but giggle at her father,
he always was looking out for her. The
conversation was kept short, as Annette
had dinner waiting on the table, and Ann
felt her own stomach growl. Ann hung up
the call with her father, ordering room
service. She was quite content to be in her
pajamas, having no desire to get dressed
again and drive anywhere to find dinner.

   The overlarge Cobb salad and sweet
tea hit the spot, Ann was shocked when
she realized she had eaten the entire
platter of salad watching the news on the
war in Iraq. More IED's and terrorist
attacks had taken the lives of ten U.S.
service members, injuring dozens more.
The news was depressing anytime Ann
watched it, but it always hit close to home
when a service member died. Digging

through her purse, Ann pulled out Logan's letter, carefully tearing the top open.

Dear Ann,

I'm doing good, how're you? Thanks for the Christmas box, the guys in the shop really liked the candy. I'm not much Into candy, but I appreciate the thought. You can always send cookies, chocolate chip are my favorite. You can't ever go wrong with cakes, cookies and pies with me.

Most folks don't get what I do, don't expect them to either. It's all I've really known for the last almost twelve years now, this Navy life. It has its good and bad points, but at least I won't have to worry about looking for a job for a while, I plan on retiring out of the Navy. Maybe once I retire I'll just ride my horses and motorcycle and hunt for a bit, just to get all this out of my system. Yeah, it's kinda fucked up that the nationals have us fix their shit and then the next day they're trying to kill us. I don't get it, but I knew

*when I signed my name it wasn't gonna
be anything easy.*

*Oh yeah, 120 is almost the norm
every day. I don't worry about heat
exhaustion as much as I worry about
dehydration. Lots of my guys fall out
cause of dehydration. Most of us that work
hard and are outside in the heat wear a
Camelback. It's kinda like a backpack with
a gallon or two of water in it, and a hose
with a suction end on it that you can drink
from. I usually wear one when I'm out on
a project or a convoy, not usually when
I'm working in the shop though. Don't
want it tore up when I'm under a machine
or get me hung up in a machine.*

*So you come from a farm? Are you
talking a real farm with acreage or one of
those hobby farms that are real tiny? That
makes me feel better that I'm talking with
someone who probably can understand me
a bit better than others. I got twenty acres
out in Colorado up in the mountains near
Cascade that my house sits on. It's just a
little two bedroom one bath cabin, but it
does me well enough. I got a couple*

horses to go with it all, but don't call me a cowboy darlin', I'm just a country boy from Clayton, GA. I love being up in the Rockies though, it's similar to GA but different too. I see it as my long term place to land.

Good for you going to college, especially medical school. I guess if I get hurt when I get back to the states I need to give you a shout huh? You'll do well as a doctor, with your want of helping people. I'm not smart enough to do the college thing, but the Navy says if I want to make Senior Chief that I need to get a four year degree in something. I don't know if I want to do that yet. I ain't like all these fat coffee swilling officers and wanna be officers. I still work for a living, and I ain't afraid of getting dirty neither.

I get you when you say people make fun of the way you talk, they do it to me here sometimes too. I think a GA accent on a woman is sexy, guess it's just part of where I grew up, girl's downhome sure know how to talk to a man, that's for sure. Sounds like your family are real good people, just like you. Your folks did it right with ya Ann, you don't gotta send me the boxes, but I sure do appreciate them and your letters too. You don't know how much it means to me when I see mail from you, to know that someone somewhere gives a shit about me.

My brother, Butch, he's older than me, he's been in and outta jail so much that I think last I knew he was locked up in Jacksonville, NC, for some stupid shit he got into with a motorcycle club he was in. I don't know much about it, but Butch's better off in the jail- trust me.

I really liked the cds you sent, most of them are stuff I like and listen to often. I never heard of the opera guy though, but I find that when I listen to him singing it calms me down, I usually listen to him at night while I'm gearing down from the day. I got about halfway through the book, I'll probably finish it before we come home in the summer. Have you read it? It's not like anything I'm used to reading, but it's still pretty interesting. Can't think of nothing I really want you to send me in a box, guess just whatever you think. I'm sure I'll like whatever you send.

Doesn't make me feel weird that you're praying for me, but while you're praying for me send one up for my guys over here too will ya? They go outside the wire and help make things better here, risking their lives every day to keep freedom free for you and everyone else back home. We don't get much in thank you's over here, probably 'cause there ain't much here to start with. Thank you Ann for keeping me in your thoughts, means a lot to me.

I gotta get going, I'm grimy and sweaty from working and I really want a shower before bed. I hope you had a good Christmas with your family, and a good New Year.

Take Care,

Logan

Ann panicked when she realized that her tears had splashed onto the paper, she tried brushing them off with her fingertips, only to smudge the dark pencil strokes.

"Shit!" Ann sighed, setting the letter down and wiping her eyes with the neck of her t-shirt. Getting herself composed, Ann pulled out her notebook that she usually used to write observation notes in when she was at the clinical sites. Her hand flew across the pages, front and back, replying to Logan's letter as the tears threatened to fall more. She had to get the reply that was in her heart out before it left her, making sure she would get it out in the mail first thing in the morning.

Writing the reply back to Logan brought peace to Ann's travel weary soul, it wasn't long after she laid down that Ann was lost in the darkness of sleep.

Chapter Seven

"Dixon! Anybody seen Chief Dixon!" YNSN Simmons yelled through the shop, seeing heads turn at her voice. None of the faccs belonged to Chief Dixon, Simmons didn't have the guts to go knock on the Goat Locker door --not that Dixon would be there anyway. Dixon was known for not being part of the good ol' boys Chief club who hung out in the Goat Locker. If he was anywhere, he could be found elbow deep in grease and oil inside a piece of equipment.

"Come on guys! Any of you know where Chief is?" Simmons was getting pretty annoyed at this point, seeing heads shake and no sign of Dixon.

"Fucking Simmons! Give me whatever it is you got for Chief, I'll take it to him!" Mels' gruff voice made Simmons balk as she handed the box and letter over to the clearly pissed off and dirty female lead mechanic, before making a hasty retreat from CM1 Heiderschiedt.

Mels snorted in laughter, seeing who both pieces of mail were from. Was Logan seeing this girl or was he just leading her on to get a box of goodies now and then? Mels didn't know what the story was, but this was the third box that came from this Ann Stranahan in Elmsford, NY for him. Mels barked at CM2 Johnson to take over, that she was going out give Chief his mail and get some chow. Johnson just nodded, turning back to the hydraulic system on the loader that had blew on the last project sitting in front of him.

Mels walked through the maze of buildings that comprised most of Camp Fallujah. She passed the galley, medical, and the admin offices heading for Logan's quarters. Mels' fingers punched in the code automatically, the blast of cool air coming out of the door shocking her face. Mels shut the door behind her, seeing Logan sprawled out across the bed in nothing put a pair of PT shorts. Operatic music filled the confines of the small room, making Mels scrunch her nose in disgust. Usually Logan would wake at the slightest noise, not this day. Logan was snoring deeply as Mels sat down in his desk chair, looking at Logan's sleep softened features.

Logan needed to take care of his dog face before night muster. The higher ups switched him to the night crew, as Chief Stephens had a heart attack two weeks ago, earning himself a one way flight home via Landsthul once the Corpsman had him stabilized. That put Mels in charge of the day shift as Leading Petty Officer, while Logan flopped over to nights. Mels smirked, the heart attack oughta teach Stephens to lay off the coffee and donuts and get his fat ass out to PT more than once a year.

"Logan…" Mels called from the safety of the desk, watching for signs of him rousing. "Logan get your ass up, ya got fuckin' mail!" Mels' long muscled right leg stretched out, the toe of her boot expeditiously kicking Logan's fingertips none too gently.

Logan's eyes shot open as he yelled out, rolling out of the bed onto his feet.

His eyes softened at seeing Mels, a shaky hand running over his hair and face before a smirk formed at the corner of his lips. Logan sunk back down onto the edge of the bed, his body immediately relaxing.

"What the fuck Mels? I'm trying to get some fucking sleep before I go in. What's so goddamned important you gotta wake me up?" Logan huffed, taking a long drink of the water bottle beside the bed, his eyes tracking over Mels with interest.

Mels glance dropped to Logan's lap, her eyes transfixed on the impressive show of morning wood that Logan was unapologetically sporting. She knew all too well what he could do with that, memories of Apra Harbor hitting Mel's full force in her chest, sinking in between her thighs.

"What? Ya come here to help me out or we just dancing again?" Logan growled lowly, his hand reaching into his shorts to adjust the painful erection straining against the thin fabric of the PT gear.

"Fuck you Logan! It isn't like that anymore and you know it. Here." Mels dropped the mail in his lap, bee-lining out the door. She took a deep breath at hearing Logan's door click shut behind her. Mels knew that look in Logan's bedroom eyes better than anyone, and before whatever came of it ended up hurting her heart, she bolted. He'd already turned her down at Christmas, and that had wounded Mels deep. She wasn't about to be his mid-day tryst and get turned down later on, it just wasn't fair. It was all or nothing in Melanie Heiderschiedt's mind. Mels headed for the galley, eating sounded better than anything right now.

Logan grumbled something about Mels not having a fucking clue as he flipped the letter over. The box he knew who it was from, but a single letter could be anything. Surprise lit his face when he realized the letter and the box were both from Ann, this was a new twist on the friendship by mail.

Logan cut the seams on the box, finding a Ziploc bag with a pale blue material inside. In Ann's neat script were the words "Open Me" written on the bag with Sharpie. Logan's curiosity got the best of him, separating the seams of the bag slowly. That same floral scent that was light on the pages of her previous letters was on the material in the bag. Pulling it out of the bag, Logan realized it was a pillowcase, the material soft and slick between his fingers. Nothing like the rough cotton of the sheets currently on his bed. He put the pillowcase back in the bag, sealing it up. Digging through the box, he found more bathroom items and eight more bags of chocolate chip cookies.

In the bottom of the box was a pink envelope, Logan ran his thumbnail under the seam. A notecard fell into his lap, along with a photo, his eyes darted to the photo, pulling it out of his lap. In the photo was a beautiful woman in surgical scrubs. Blonde hair pulled back into a pony tail, a sweet smile on her face. The big blue eyes were what pulled him in, he couldn't take his eyes off of her. Was this Ann? Logan flipped over the notecard, her handwriting clear in between the lines.

Keep half the cookies for you, share the rest with your guys. Thought you needed more bathroom stuff. The pillowcase is to keep the lonely thoughts at bay. I hope you like what you see in me. Ann

Logan picked up the photo again, studying Ann's features. She looked just about how he pictured her in his day dream of her out in the mountains of Colorado with him. Ann looked so young compared to him, but she had to be at least 24 if she was in her last few years of medical school. If this was going to go anywhere, he needed to know from her how old she was. She was more beautiful than any woman he'd been with prior, that was apparent. Logan packed the box back up, putting it on his desk. He kept the photo and notecard, opening up the lone letter and laying back on his bed to read it. Ann's scent lingering in the pages, as his eyes scanned her floral script.

Logan,

I hope this letter finds you well. I just about missed your letter that you sent to my parents' house. Daddy gave it to me as I was driving out of the farm, it put a smile on my face nonetheless. You're welcome for the candy, I'm glad your guys enjoyed it. I guess I'll send you cookies in your next box for you, and you better keep some for yourself!

So I'm sitting in a hotel room near Richmond, VA writing you. I was watching the news and saw where some Seabees from Camp Fallujah had been injured by an IED. I can't lie and say I didn't think about you and hope and pray it wasn't you. I couldn't help but cry, please God don't let one of those injured guys be you. I know you say it's all part of what you signed your name for, but I can't help but to care about you and how you are doing.

I come from a real farm to answer your question. Our farm has been in our family since the turn of the century, when

Great Grandpa Stranahan bought it with gold when he came over from Ireland. We have horses, cattle and other small livestock. I ride my mare Nellie whenever I am home. I think it's something to be proud of that you have a house with land in Colorado. And no, I wouldn't call you a cowboy, especially if you are from Georgia. Maybe sometime I can come out to Colorado and we can go riding and see the Rockies? I've never been west of the Mississippi, so Colorado would be something new to me. Clayton is about five hours from my parents place, you're from up there in the mountains. I bet it's beautiful up there.

Don't ever cut yourself down saying you're not smart enough to go to college! You can do it, all you have to do is try! It's admirable that you are apart from your peers and aren't afraid to get dirty and work. Thank you for supporting me going to medical school, not many people do. I fully expect you to be one of my patients when you get back to the states. I can promise you quality healthcare in my hands.

So a GA girl accent turns you on? Well, I guess it's safe for me to admit a GA guy's accent does things to me as well. If we ever get to meet, it's going to be awkward with us both getting turned on by the other talking right? LOL. I'd like to meet you someday, that way I can at least put a face with the name of the person I've been praying for all these nights.

You're welcome for the boxes and the stuff I put in them, it's the least I can do for someone giving up so much and being so far from home. I can kinda relate to the loneliness, sometimes I go days without hearing from anyone up at school. I guess that's why I look forward to mail from you, that way it reminds me that someone else feels just like I do. Sure I go to class and clinical, but it's not the same kind of interaction that you get from someone you love, so it's not as fulfilling. I don't even have a boyfriend for cripes sakes, or a dog. So I come home to an empty apartment, and that's just depressing. I can't imagine what it's like for you, but I know thinking about it makes me sad.

I'm glad you like the Bocelli disc, I listen to it too when I want to relax. Ha, the book—yeah I've gotten about halfway through it as well. My friend Leah bought it for me, and it's not what I usually read either, but it's good. I'm glad we seem to like the same kind of music, that way I know what else to send you. I'll try and figure out some different stuff to send you in my next box, expect cookies though!

I definitely will keep praying for you and your guys to stay safe. I really appreciate what you're doing over there, even if it only has a small impact on our lives over here. Thank you so much for keeping watch while I sleep, it makes me feel better knowing you're over there taking care of things. I have faith that you can fix everything that's needed and make things run smoothly.

I need to get to bed, it's late and I have the other half of the drive to get home to New York tomorrow. I hope you write back, but if you can would you please email me? That way we don't miss each other letters by chance.

Take Care,

Ann

Logan took note of the NYMC.edu email address at the bottom of the page, grabbing the photo and notecard before he got out of bed to go to his desk. The words of Ann's letter touched him deep, she understood more about him than he thought she would. Logan snapped off a bit of medical tape out of the crash kit hanging off his gear, tacking the picture of Ann up to lamp on his desk near his laptop. He looked up in those soulful blue eyes, sighing. His laptop beeped as it powered up, Logan wasn't getting anymore sleep before going into work tonight. He might as well spend that time emailing Ann back, since she took the time out of her trip to write him her emotionally charged letter. Logan needed to vent to someone, and Mels wasn't the someone he wanted at the moment.

Chapter Eight

Ann was sitting in the hospital break room, doodling with her notebook and pencil. She was drawing pictures of roses, but her mind kept falling back to thoughts of Logan. She hadn't heard from him since the letter her father gave her a month ago as she was leaving the farm, and that letter had been almost two weeks old at that point. She had sent Logan a letter she wrote in Virginia, and then when she got home to New York she sent him another box with cookies. Inside that same box was a picture Leah took of her when they did their clinical rotations at the children's hospital. Ann was apprehensive as hell sending him that photo, but she was sure he was just as curious about what she looked like as she was about him. Curiosity had gotten the best of her, she had even Googled "CMC Logan Dixon United States Navy" and came up with text articles about projects he worked on and awards he had received. Ann came up empty handed on the pictures, which made her even more curious about him. He had a fair amount of awards and citations attached to his name in the Navy articles she read, but instead of Googling what those meant, she thought it would be better to ask him herself.

Ann jumped at the bottle of Coke immediately invading her personal space. She looked up to see her best friend Leah drape herself over the chair across from Ann. How Leah made it look so effortless and sexy to be in a break room chair like that, Ann would never know she did it. Leah never had a problem with getting a date, Ann couldn't get a date in New York. They were two completely different women, but that was what made them best friends.

"Hey Anners, how you doin? You look depressed or some shit. How's your man in Iraq doing?" Leah had been worried about Ann, since returning from Christmas break she had become more invested in school than was probably healthy for her and not going out with friends. Leah was genuinely worried for her bestie, this last month of behavior was out of the norm for Ann.

Ann smiled at the concern Leah showed for Logan's well-being, that proved to Ann that even her best friend was of the mind that Logan and Ann were an item. Ann figured it would just be best to let Leah think what she wanted, because who knew what would come of all of it?

Ann unscrewed the top on the Coke, taking a long drink before passing it to Leah who shook her head. "Nah, I bought it for you. You look like you could use the caffeine. So I saw on the news awhile back some Seabees got injured near Fallujah, I hope that wasn't Logan's guys. Have you heard anything from him?"

"I got a letter when I was leaving home from break. That letter was ten days old, so I hope he's okay. I haven't heard from him since, and I sent him another box of cookies and a letter I wrote when I was in Virginia. Tom at the post office told me mail can take longer if he's off the base out at a project. I hope and pray he wasn't with those guys that got hurt, that would be terrible. I gave him my email address in my last letter that I put with the box of cookies and a picture of me. I haven't seen an email from him either." Ann sighed as she took another drink of the ice cold Coke; she really hoped Logan wasn't with the guys that got hurt, and if he was she hoped he wasn't injured. Not hearing from him and seeing that on the news had made her pray even more for Logan and his guys.

"You sent a pic of yourself? Have you seen him yet? I hope he wasn't with those guys that got injured either. I kinda picture him ya know, over six foot, dark hair, and dark eyes, muscular. He's a mechanic, so he's gotta be a big guy. Maybe he's emailed you back, and it's sitting in your spam box? He's probably got some Navy email address that he's emailing you from, so maybe your email thinks its junk?" Leah licked her lips, stealing a drink from Ann's Coke.

"Leah really! I'm sure Logan looks fine, and I'm sure I'll see him soon enough in pictures. You are a genius! I'll check my spam box when I get home. Tell Dr. Rivers

I'll make up the rest of my time later this week." Ann jumped out of her seat; skipping over to her best friend and wrapping her arms around her. "I love you! Can we do dinner in and a movie tonight?" Ann kissed Leah on the cheek, smudging her lip gloss.

Leah chuckled, "Sure, I'll bring some sushi over and we can watch Boondock Saints. The two lead guys are oh my god gorgeous! Love you too hun. See you about seven?"

Ann nodded, heading out the break room door with a skip in her step. She wanted to get home and check her email.

Ann sat at her computer with a towel around her head, her hair was soaking wet from the shower. Anytime Ann worked in the ER she always took a shower as soon as she got home, you never knew if you could have blood on you that you didn't know about. She logged into her school portal and into her mailbox, clicking the spam folder. Leah was right, in the box sat an email from a "CMC Dixon, Logan" dated two weeks ago. Which meant in another two days the server would have swept her spam box clean. Ann clicked the link that flagged the email address as 'not spam' and the email was moved to her inbox.

Backing out to her inbox, Ann saw there were attachments to the email, wondering what they were. Opening the email, Ann started to read as she took a drink from the glass of water on her desk.

Hey Ann,

Yeah you're right, email is a good idea. I'd hate for us to miss each other by the mail, especially with mail being so hit or miss over here. Glad your Daddy gave you my letter, glad to hear it made you smile. That makes me feel good. It's kinda my bright moment in hell when I see mail from you, it always makes me smile.

About the news, unless you hear it's my specific battalion don't worry about me. I know the guys that got hurt, they weren't mine, and they were from a battalion that was coming in for a repair to their armadillo. It's a bad thing when someone gets hurt over here, cause if it's bad enough they get sent back to the states on a one way ticket through Germany. I've been lucky to not get hurt like that. I've had the usual busted fingers and cuts, but nothing what them boys went through. If you're really worried about me, and I know this is gonna sound bad, but don't watch the news. I'll have you put on the call list with the ombudsman, and she will let you know if something really bad happens to me ok? Don't worry about me, I've been through this before, and I've lived through worse. I'll be ok, promise ya that.

Even better that you come from a real farm and you ride darlin'. Means I ain't gotta worry about you on horseback when we go out in the mountains. I'll take us up to this little place I know not too far from Pikes Peak. It's just this meadow near a finger river, we can fish and camp. I go up there and camp when I want to be away from the world. Just me and the wilderness, I can hunt and fish and have quiet. It's beautiful up there with the green grass and the wildflowers. Closest I've been to heaven out there in the Rockies. Your farm sounds like a real nice place, I wouldn't mind seeing it sometime. That's something to be proud of that your farm has been in your family so long. A legacy is something to be proud of, especially one like that.

I'll think about going to college, but I ain't making any promises. I don't necessarily need a college degree to make Senior Chief, my evals are usually pretty alright. It would just help seal the deal a little better. Hell, I'm the first one in my immediate family who's even finished high school. My brother got a GED to get into the Army back when I was a kid. I'll support you finishing medical school, that's something to be proud of Ann, getting to be a doctor. You'll be pretty well off when that happens, and I'll still be turning wrenches here for the Navy. I'll be able to say I knew you before you got rich and famous, when I was still nobody.

Yup, something about the way women in GA talk, it makes me just kinda go stupid for a minute. Glad to know I'm not the only one that happens to, so I guess if we ever get the chance to talk there'll be a few minutes of silence between us. My roommate is from Minnesota, and while sometimes that accent is sexy, it can get annoying too. I'd like to meet you sometime, maybe after I get back we can get together somehow?

Thanks for the cookies in your box. I split them with the guys in my shop, they always look forward to goodies from home. I don't know what to say about the pillowcase, it's really soft and I'm guessing it smells like you on purpose? If you did that on purpose, thanks. I have it on the other pillow on my bed and it makes me think about you and that you worry and care for me over there. I always can use bathroom stuff.

Maybe you need to get a dog? Sorry I can't help in the boyfriend department, being half a world away. Getting mail from you helps with the loneliness, and sometimes I get really busy over here with work and all that I don't have time to be lonely. It gets easier, especially when I hear from you.

I appreciate your prayers for me and my guys, every little bit helps when you're so far from home. I knew when I signed my name all those years ago it wouldn't be easy and I would do things like I have. But I only got another 8 years left and I can retire.

Darlin' I'm gonna say this and please don't take it the wrong way, but how old are you? I think you're beautiful. I never seen a woman as pretty as you. Don't ever think you're not beautiful--I'm the one who's an ugly son of a bitch.

Gonna stop here. I gotta head into work; they got me working the night shift since the night Chief had a heart attack and got sent home one way through Germany. Thanks for thinking of me and all, I really do appreciate it.

Have a good night,

Logan

Ann clicked the three files attached to the email, waiting to see what they were. Her breath caught in her throat when the file popped up on her screen, it was a photo. Wearing a black leather jacket and a grey t-shirt, it looked like Logan was sitting on a chair at someone's house. His dirty blonde hair was messy, and it looked like he had about a week or so growth on his face. His piercing blue eyes burned right through Ann, she felt a flutter in her abdomen. He was so very good looking, why did this man not have a wife? Surely he had an ex-wife? The next picture was one of him standing against what looked like the back of a truck in combat gear, a pair of sunglasses on his face under a uniform hat, holding a rifle. There was a smile on his face, and Ann guessed it was because of the "Colorado or Bust" sign written with Sharpie on a piece of cardboard duct taped over his left shoulder.

Ann giggled at the sign, but was still entranced by Logan's rugged good looks in uniform. There was no way in the world he was interested in her, he was easily 29 maybe? Ann didn't know. The last picture was amazing, it was a sunset over what she assumed was the camp that Logan lived in in Iraq. It made Ann forget that he was even in a warzone, with it being so beautiful.

Ann saved the photos to her desktop, knowing Leah would be over before too long. Now she had a face to go with the man, and he was surely easy on the eyes. Ann's heart began to beat quicker as she got up to finish drying her hair, those blue eyes haunting her.

Chapter Nine

Logan looked at his watch, knowing with it being 0200 in Colorado that Ann would be getting up to get ready for clinical. At least that's what he thought to himself, as the heat bore down outside the walls of the tent city they were living in at the current project at Baharia. This project was a big one, the Seabees were essentially building a base for US troops to work out of in the war on terror. This was what Seabees did best, building a fully functioning base out of nothing. The Seabees had been working through the wars since 1942, building and fighting. The Seabees might be the lesser known red headed stepchild of the Navy, but they got shit done when they were called up.

The last few days were pushing 140 degrees by the lake, Logan would have loved to strip down and jump in the water to cool off. But that was against the regs of course. At least when it was hot as hell out, work was called off a little early, which left Logan with plenty of idle time, without computer access. Mail would come, but only if a convoy brought it out, which meant that any mail Ann sent would be beat all to hell and two weeks old if not more. He wondered why she hadn't replied to the email he sent with the pictures before the convoy headed out. Did she think he was that ugly? Or maybe she thought he was too old for her? Thoughts of reasons for rejections swirled in his brain, kicking him in the gut. Ann was a beautiful woman, even if she was younger than him.

"Hey Chief, what time is it?" A feminine voice roused Logan out of his thoughts, looking to his left seeing HMC Tate walking towards him, a med kit slung over her shoulder and a grin on her face. She walked up to stand next to Logan, jabbing him in the ribs with her elbow. "You been looking at that watch a bit too long pal, you feeling ok? You know why I'm here and what I gotta do. Your quarters or mine?"

Hospital Corpsman Chief Bonnie Tate had been with 17 since Logan had reported on, at that point she was an HM1, back five years ago. Tate was a whiz when it came to medicine, last Logan had talked to her she was considering medical school once she was out of the Navy. If Logan had to go to war with any "Doc" he'd take Tate every time over the men. She was fiercely loyal, tough as nails and put her ass on the line to take care of her 'Bees. That was what Logan admired about her; she took medicine seriously, and knew more than was taught at Corpsman school.

Logan smirked, eyes cutting to the stocky, dark haired farmer's daughter from back East. She was one of the boys in a woman's body; Logan knew she had a girlfriend back home in Colorado waiting on her. As much as it was against Don't Ask Don't Tell; Logan wasn't bothered by who Tate loved, and as long as it didn't interfere with her work it wasn't nothing to get pissed off about.

"Well I guess Chief, since you put it that way, your place is a whole lot comfier than mine. Even with your CASH stull in progress of being built." Logan knew Tate would pick up on the smart ass in his voice; he was waiting for the return fire.

"Well if you slow pokes would stop fucking around, jerking off with your peckers in your hand I would have a fully functioning CASH by now. Fuckers need to get moving and get on it or y'all are gonna be getting the silver bullet from me!" And there was the Tate that Logan loved, she never missed a beat.

A grin spread across Logan's face as he followed Tate over to the CASH, knowing it was time for the brash "Doc" to do his mid-deployment med screen. He was glad it was Tate, any of the other Corpsmen made him edgy, most likely because he didn't know them as well as he knew Tate.

Logan closed the door behind them after he stepped into the exam room, shucking off his t-shirt before hopping up on the exam table. He breathed a sigh of relief seeing Bonnie flip open his file, sitting down at her desk.

"You been feeling ok Logan? Any thoughts of suicide? Hurting yourself or others? Any depressing thoughts?" Bonnie's voice was clinical, but not cold. Logan was close to the Doc, she was his go to when things with Mels would go shit.

"Naw. Not gonna kill myself, might beat the shit out of some of these CMCN's. Fuckin' dumb kids right out of Hueneme." Logan caught eyes with Bonnie as she came up with her otoscope and stethoscope. He knew well enough that Bonnie could do the exam without thinking about it, Logan seized the opportunity to get some things off his chest.

"Hey Bonnie, can we talk while you check me over? Got something on my mind and you know some shit I can't talk with H-12 about." Logan's voice was almost a whisper as the cool metal of the stethoscope touched the skin of his back, Bonnie never commented on his scars or asked him about them. That was why Logan trusted her, she didn't need to be told anything he didn't want to tell her, she just *knew*.

"Logan you know you can always come to me. Nothing ever leaves these ears, you know that as well as anyone." Bonnie listened to Logan's heart and lungs, then checked his spine and muscles. She always took longer with the people she was close to, because they usually needed to talk as well.

"Bonnie, I think I'm getting feelings for a woman back in the states. She got my name and address here off a Holidays for Heroes tree at her church and we've been writing letters, and she's been sending boxes since about Thanksgiving. This last box that came before we left Fallujah she sent me a picture of her. And she's beautiful, kinda reminds me of your Jaye. Blonde and blue. Well, anyways I emailed her this long email a week or so before we left base and I haven't heard back. I sent her pics of me and let my heart talk for me. She's been sounding like she's getting feelings for me, but she's sounding like she's scared to out and out say it. I'm worried I said the wrong fucking thing and she's turned tail and run." Logan's voice trembled, he sat up a bit straighter when Bonnie's warm hand laid on his shoulder, squeezing slightly.

"Logan, you know that we don't have email access out here, and mail runs like shit 'cause it has to be brought to us. You only know this gal by mail, and that's fine. Shit, that's how my Grandparents fell in love during the war. I'm sure she thinks you're a good looking cuss, and that your email box is waiting with messages in it and there's probably some mail sitting in the shop for you when we get back to Fallujah. If you feel the need to write her get out your notebook and pencil and just write. That's what I do when I can't hear from Jaye. I write in my notebook like I'm writing to her. Just let your heart talk Logan, I'm sure this gal would appreciate it. And when we get back to Fallujah, put those pages in the mail or into an email. I'm here if you need me anytime." Bonnie was the sister Logan wished he had, she knew how to talk to him without talking down to him. As much as she was a hard ass on the outside, she was soft on the inside.

"Thanks Doc, I knew you would know what to say to make me feel better. You always do. So do I pass your inspection? Or do you need to shoot me and put me out of my misery?" Logan smirked, pulling his t-shirt back over his head, knowing Bonnie didn't go through the entire screen she should have. Not that he would have cared if she'd palpated his guts or his groin, it was all clinical anyways.

"Yeah, I'll let ya skate Logan. But seriously, sit and write her. It'll make you feel better. Always makes me feel better when I can't talk to Jaye. She always has a lot to say when those mile long letters and emails come through." Bonnie signed off on Logan's chart, having him read it and initial before he turned to leave.

"I mean it, thanks Doc, for everything." Logan smiled slightly at the woman looking at him with playful green eyes.

"Get your mangy ass the fuck outta here Dixon. You know neither of us do mushy well." Bonnie laughed as she chucked a roll of gauze at Logan, pegging him in the face as the door closed.

Logan needed somewhere quiet to be with his thoughts, somewhere where no one else would bother him. There was a crew building a heavy artillery gun casement on the base, and a crew working on finishing up the CASH. There weren't many places Logan could go to get privacy, with so much work going on through the day and night. He knew Bonnie was right when she suggested that he sat down and write out his feelings. Logan seemed to be able to express his feelings better in written word rather than spoken word. He always had trouble putting his feelings into spoken word, probably due in part to how he grew up.

Logan stood in the middle of the compound, seeing his guys relaxing under a tent with a cooler of what could be maybe considered ice and a clear plastic tub on the ground that they gathered around. Logan walked over, fishing out a bottle of cool water from the dingy water that the ice was becoming, wiping the top off on his t-shirt.

"What's the show today?" Logan sidled up to CM2 Johnson, taking a drink from the bottle. There wasn't much for entertainment out in the desert that wouldn't get them into trouble. It was too hot for rugby or volleyball, and it wasn't like they could go swim in the lake, not knowing what was living in the water. It was rumored that the lake was full of the dead bodies of prostitutes that the Hussein sons murdered when they grew tired of them. The thought pissed Logan off that women were looked down on the way they were in this country. He was glad that Mels was back in Fallujah where she was safe, and he wasn't ever going to mention this atrocity to Ann.

Johnson looked down into the tub full of sand and rocks, watching the two creatures circle in the confined space. "Looks like a camel spider vs. a scorpion. What's your bet Boss?" The CM's had their own version of 'Deadliest Warrior' while in Iraq, even if it was with the local insect population.

Logan shrugged, "I'll give it to the camel spider. Them fuckers are carnivorous as hell." It was true, the spiders while not being much bigger than the palm of your hand, had a powerful bite that hurt like a son of a bitch. Bonnie had treated a few of the guys for a bite from the spider. It wasn't poisonous, just painful. The spider was infamous for eating other small bugs and small animals out in the desert. People back home thought they were huge and poisonous, but that was all started as an urban legend.

"Yeah, I don't think the scorpion will last, but fuck it. It's better than watching the wind blow." Johnson tossed his empty water bottle into the tub, making the scorpion jump back a few inches.

"You let me know who wins. I'm gonna go get some downtime." Logan tucked his water bottle into the pocket of his cammies, heading out for the line of trucks sitting idle in the lot. If something went down and he was needed Logan knew Johnson would come find him.

Crawling up into the cab of the stake truck, Logan reached into the pocket of his cammies, pulling out the bottle of water, his moleskine notebook and a nubby little pencil that had seen better days. Logan took a deep breath as the pencil began moving across the dirty worn pages, the words flowing from his heart to Ann on paper.

Chapter Ten

Logan couldn't sleep. He jerked awake with a strangled yell, sweat pouring off his skin despite the a/c unit running in his quarters in Fallujah. Stumbling out of bed, he stripped off his shorts and crawled into the shower. He was careful not to wake her, knowing she had to go into work in a couple of hours.

Since getting back from Baharia, Logan couldn't sleep alone. He would wake up gasping for air, sweating with his heart racing. He knew if he went to medical they would either dope him up or send him home depending upon who saw him that day. Neither was a choice he was willing to take, he wasn't going to leave his guys hanging. Logan had a job to do. He would fix himself the best he could and carry on smartly, that's what Seabees did when shit hit the fan.

Things seemed to fall into place when he walked into his quarters off the convoy and found Mels in his bed asleep.

Logan stripped off his gear, down to nothing but his underwear leaving a pile of clothes on the floor. He crawled into the bed next to Mels, wrapping her up in his arms, curling his battered and weary body around her. Mels didn't say a word that night, she pulled Logan closer to her and let him fight his way to sleep. Logan appreciated the quiet between them, Mels' intuition kicking in and letting things lie.

Mels was Logan's best friend, she had his back no matter what was going on. Whether it was a bar fight, getting the new guy straight or running errands for him while he was at work, Mels handled it. She might have once been his lover, but that was behind them now. This bond was one that Logan needed in his life, someone he could lean on when he couldn't handle the weight. Mels was a better sibling than Butch ever was, he'd trade Mels over Butch any day of the week and that was saying something.

Logan stood in the shower, the tepid water running down his tanned skin, his scattered thoughts slowly coming together. He hadn't checked his email since getting back to base three days ago, he hadn't even went looking for mail from Ann in the shop either. Simmons hadn't sought Logan out, and the pillowcase had long lost Ann's sweet scent. Grumbling to himself, Logan turned the water off standing in his quarters naked. He grabbed the towel off the back of the desk chair, briskly drying his body.

He pulled out a fresh set of uniform parts, dressing in the dark. Mels was still sound asleep in the bed, the gentle swell of one breast peeking out of the sheets. She could never sleep in a shirt, more often than not she slept naked when they were home in Colorado. Here in Iraq, when she slept in her own quarters, she wore a t-shirt and shorts to bed. Logan wasn't the least bit surprised she was only clad in a pair of shorts in his bed. He needed that human contact, needed something that was real and not someone who was half a world away and only existed via mail and emails.

Logan hit the power button on his computer, gathering up the items he would need for work today. He was back on the night shift since coming back from Baharia, his sleep was completely fucked up and his temper was getting harder to keep in check. There wasn't a safe outlet for the emotions boiling within him, even though he knew Mels wouldn't have anything against him unleashing on her, they weren't that way anymore.

Logan heard his email pinging, he slid into the desk chair clicking the icon flashing on the screen. There were the usual emails about his bills getting paid by the bank through e-bill, the specials for Cabellas for that month along with an email from Ann that was now almost a month old. Had he really been gone on the Baharia project for a month? Time had slipped through his fingers, and he hadn't even been aware. Logan's fingers trembled over the mouse, hovering over the subject line. What if it was Ann telling him she wasn't interested in around about way? What if she was interested in him?

What ifs were going to kill him, he needed to just ball up and click.

Logan expelled the breath he wasn't aware he was holding as his eyes began reading through Ann's reply.

Hey Logan,

God I feel so much better knowing it wasn't you with those guys that got hurt! It's still heartbreaking to know that some were killed and injured. War is such a terrible place, and I worry about you so very much. I cried when I read that you were okay. You don't have to put me on the call list, but if you want to, I'll put my number at the end of this email. I won't watch the news anymore, it's just so depressing and it makes me worry about you even more.

That place you described out by Pikes Peak sounds beautiful. I'd love to fish in the river and see if I can catch anything. I know how to fish, I'm just not very good at it. I've been camping with my family before, so that would be nice to go on a horseback getaway with you and just forget the world for a few days. If you're still comfortable with it when you get back, we should definitely plan it out. I have this coming summer off, and don't have plans. I'd love to see Colorado, I've heard so much about the West and yet I've never really been anywhere except the states between New York and Georgia when I'm driving between home and school. I guess I could always fly out there and have you pick me up at the airport? We'll see how things go while you're gone as to what will happen when you get back to the states.

That's something to be proud of to be the first person in your immediate family to finish high school. I'm really proud of you for that one, and I'll stand beside you if you decide to go to college. I guess I'll be ok financially once I pay off the $100k of school loans from med school, but until then I'm still going to be poor little Ann Stranahan. You're not nobody Logan, you couldn't ever be nobody. Not to me. You're a great guy *who's done so much with his life past the little mountain town of Clayton. At least you're doing better than your brother, you're not in jail. I couldn't imagine going to jail, my Daddy went a couple of times because he got drunk. That was before I was born though, when my sister's mother died. Daddy just kind of went crazy for a bit, and Krista went and stayed with Grandma and Grandpa Stranahan in Florida until Daddy got himself straight.*

I'm sure there will be moments of silence when we talk to each other, if we ever get to that point. I didn't know you had a roommate? Is it your roommate in Iraq or at your house in Colorado? Is he a mechanic like you? Is he Navy as well? Sorry if I'm being pushy, I'm just curious as you've never mentioned having a roommate before. Not that it matters anything to me, I'm sure living in Colorado isn't cheap and a roommate helps with the bills and such.

I'll try and get you some cookies out soon, I'm busy with school since Spring Break is coming soon. So I can't promise that I will get any out until after break. I'll be in Georgia with my family over break, my older sister Krista is marrying her fiancé Ryan. He's a really great guy, they met up at UGA the year Krista went up there and tried college. She ended up coming home and Ryan came with her. That's love, giving up everything and everyone you know for someone you love and moving a good distance away for that person. And I'm in the wedding of course! Krista has already bought my shoes and dress, all I need to do is show up and get pretty! It's at the family farm, so I'm sure there will be loads of people there. But I'll be going solo, if you were home I would totally ask you to go with me. I'm sure you look handsome in your dress uniform!

I wasn't aware that the pillowcase smelled like me? I probably don't smell it since I'm used to smelling it every day, but I'm glad you liked it and it helps to keep the lonely thoughts at bay. That was my intention with it, to give you something of mine to put your mind somewhere else when you're feeling low. Keep it with you and think of me when

you're feeling low, know that you're in my thoughts over here all the time.
Sometimes I wonder if you're looking up at the same sky I am and wondering what I'm doing? I catch myself doing that sometimes at night...looking up at the sky and wondering if you are okay and what you are doing. It's weird I know.

I can't get a dog, I'm never here enough to even take that great of care of myself much less a dog. Maybe if things work out between us okay while you're gone we could try the boyfriend/girlfriend by distance thing when you get back to the states? It would be easier with you in the states that way we could call and text and Skype. I don't know if you can do any of that from where you are now? I can't lie to you and say that seeing mail and emails from you doesn't put a smile on my face, especially after having a bad day. It makes me feel good that thoughts of me make you smile, I smile when I think of you.

Ok, so you're making me blush when you say I'm beautiful. I usually don't hear that unless it's from someone in my family. And to answer your question—I'm 26. But age shouldn't matter none, my parents are ten years apart in age. You can't be any more than 29 are you? My jaw dropped when I saw the pictures of you. You are not an ugly son of a bitch at all! Oh God Logan, you're so good looking and so wholesome by the words you write to me. Any woman is lucky to have you! Do you have a wife or ex-wife? Sorry for being nosey again, I just don't want to get my heart broke ya know?

Sorry to hear about the night Chief having a heart attack! I can't imagine what that was like in a warzone. Hopefully he is home with his family now and recovering. A heart attack is serious business, and can be fatal if not caught in time.

I need to get going, my friend Leah is bringing over sushi and a movie tonight. Thank you so much for emailing me back. Please take care of you and I'll keep you and your guys in my prayers.

Ann

Logan's face dropped into his hands, tears threatening to fall between his fingers. Here he was worried that Ann wouldn't want anything to do with him since he had sent her the photos and hadn't heard from her in a month. Now, from the words he read she was definitely feeling something for him, but she wasn't about to come out and say what it was. Logan could understand Ann wanting to know if there was a woman of some kind in his life, what was the point of starting someone with someone if nothing could come of it? Logan copied and pasted the phone number at the bottom of Ann's email into a blank email, sending her name, number and address off to the ombudsman of the battalion and asking for Amy to make Ann his notification in case something happened to him. Amy would do it, but he knew that an email would follow shortly asking who Ann was and why she was his notification. Logan would cross that bridge when he came to it; right now he needed to get out the door to work.

Logan heard Mels shift in her sleep; dream fueled words came out of her mouth, words he knew all too intimately. Logan reached over, brushing the hair behind Mels' ear, the small touch keeping the monsters at bay. Mels smiled, rolling over onto her side in his bed. How would Logan explain Mels? Were there words to explain their relationship without making it seem fucked up and awkward? Logan wasn't in the mood to email Ann back yet, his emotions were all over the page. Logan logged out of his email, shutting the laptop down. He needed to get a grip on things before he returned to the shop. Mels had told Logan with him being gone on the project the night Lead Mechanic wasn't getting shit done.

Logan sighed, grabbing his Oakley's and gear before heading out to the galley. Donning the Oakley's hid the war going on in Logan's eyes. Instant asshole.

Chapter Eleven

Ann wiggled into the one shade shy of crimson dress that Krista had picked out for her bridesmaid dresses, in her bedroom in front of the free standing mirror that had been Grandma Stranahan's. Red, black and old fashioned white were the colors her sister picked for the wedding, which didn't surprise Ann one bit. Krista was always the one to go for dramatic flair when it came to things like this. Ann was the one who was a bit muted when occasions like this popped up. The strappy heels would be a pain to walk through the yard with; thank God the weather had been warm and dry. Ann struggled to zip up the back of the dress, feeling her mother's gentle hands stop her shaking fingers.

"Sweetheart, relax. It's not like you're the one getting married. It's Krista and Ryan. Who knows maybe next year you and Logan will be getting married here as well?" Annette's voice floated over

Ann's bare shoulder, causing Ann to shiver.

Ann's eyes darted to her mother's as Annette came around to fix the bodice of the dress, making sure her daughter wouldn't fall out. That would be embarrassing, especially with most of the county in attendance. This was the big Spring to do in Hazlehurst, the Stranahan/Kennedy wedding.

"Mama, how do you know his name?" Ann couldn't remember telling her mother Logan's name or much about him over the last five months they had been corresponding with each other.

"Honey, Daddy and I saw his name on the letter that came for you at Christmas. It wasn't hard to figure out what's going on with him and you." Ann saw that twinkle to Annette's eye, her mother was scheming something.

Ann took her mother's hands in hers, holding that loving gaze. Ann hated to voice the words that were plaguing her heart. "Mama, I don't know what is going on with Logan and I. I haven't heard from him in a month and I think we are just friends. I have some feelings for him, but I don't know what they are exactly. So don't go getting all wedding happy for me just yet ok?"

Annette patted her daughter's arm, disappointment hidden behind her wide smile. "You'll get it figured out. Just try and be happy for Krista today please?" Ann nodded, kissing her mother on the cheek.

Ann sat down at the mirror on her desk, putting on her make up when a knock came at the door. Krista appeared in the mirror behind her, looking beautiful with her hair and makeup done. The old fashioned white dress looked gorgeous, Krista looked like she was about to break down in tears.

"Kris don't cry, it's your wedding day. You can't cry until you're pronounced

Mrs. Kennedy. I forbid it! If you cry then I will and I'll mess up my make up!" Ann threw her arms around her sister, hugging her tightly.

"Daddy'll be giving you away next year Ann, you wait and see. Is Logan doing okay over in Iraq? I know you got a letter over Christmas. But you haven't mentioned much since then." Krista's expression turned to worry, she hated seeing her little sister's heart broken. If any man hurt Ann, they would have to answer to Krista and that wasn't always a good thing. Krista was fiercely protective of Ann, ever since they were little.

"Logan's okay I guess. I haven't heard from him since the email I got about a month ago. I guess I must have said something wrong in my reply. Maybe he didn't like the picture I sent him? I don't know. It's not like we are dating or anything. He sent me some pictures of him and he's a really good looking guy though." Ann sighed at the admission that she and Logan were just friends. While she knew that someday she would like to see if there could be something between her and Logan, for now things were up in the air. It had been a month since she heard from him, something must have gone wrong.

"Oh honey, any man that doesn't think you're beautiful needs his head examined. You'll get it figured out, I have faith in you. Today, we are celebrating. So be happy ok?" Krista hugged Ann one more time, hearing Annette calling her name. Krista left Ann studying her reflection in the mirror, her thoughts on today's events. Today was about Krista, today was about family. Ann sprayed her hair one last time with hairspray, the topknot and wisps of hair falling around her face should hold most of the day.

Ann heard the band beginning to play outside, knowing that she needed to get downstairs and get into place. Snatching the bouquet of fresh flowers off her bed, Ann gathered up her dress, hurrying down the steps and out to the porch to take the arm of her groomsman. She fought back the tears as she watched

Ryan's brother Dan walk with Summer, Krista's best friend, up to their places at the altar. Dan looked so handsome in his dress uniform with the maroon beret. Dan clapped his younger brother on the shoulder, Ryan looked so nervous.

Ann took her place at the altar, seeing a space left open between Dan and Ryan's friend that Ann walked with. She was certain his name was Mike, but couldn't remember for sure. Watching through the crowd, as the ring bearer and flower girl walked up the aisle, a Marine in dress uniform walked slowly and reverently behind them. This wasn't something Ann knew about being part of the wedding, her heart clenching as she realized what was going on. The Marine carried a Marine's dress uniform crisply folded in his hands. On top of that set the formal gloves and cover, the Marine turned smartly, setting the uniform on a riser between Dan and Mike. The Marine paused, held a salute to the uniform before turning on his heel and disappearing into the crowd. At that moment, Ann heard a sob from her mother, as well as many in the crowd.

Ann spied Krista walking up with Daddy, Krista began to cry when she saw the uniform behind Dan. Daddy hugged Krista, kissing her cheek and shaking Ryan's hand as he passed off his oldest daughter to the man who would be her husband.

Ann's emotions were like a roller coaster, and the wedding was over before she was even aware. When the bridesmaids gathered to catch Krista's bouquet at the end of the ceremony, Ann was the one to catch it. Seems like everyone was in on getting her married off, but Ann was keeping her options open.

The wedding party moved to the side yard, Krista and Ryan were all smiles during the first dance. They looked truly happy, Ann was happy for them. The party settled down into people eating the barbeque and cake with some of the elderly wishing Krista and Ryan the best before they headed home. Most of the party goers left were 40 and younger, Ann being one of them. By that time of night Ann was on her fourth Jameson and Coke, and she was happy.

"Can I have this dance Miss Stranahan?" Ann looked up into the sea green eyes of Dustin Rogers. She could feel the blush rising up her face. Dustin looked every bit the cowboy; he looked great in a white button down dress shirt, dark blue Wranglers, buckle, boots and fawn colored cowboy hat.

"Uh, um, sure Dustin. I didn't know you were here! When did you get here?" Ann stammered as she took Dustin's hand, to be led out to the dance floor.

Dustin chuckled pulling Ann close, her hand in his and his hand on her lower back as they moved around the dance floor to George Strait's "That's My Kind of Woman"

"I got here just before your Daddy and Krista walked up to the altar. Krista invited me. I got stuck in traffic coming out of Macon this morning. Nice touch for Sean by the way." Dustin eased in closer to Ann as the next song started, Ann laying her head on his shoulder.

"Mmh. I don't think anyone expected that. It was beautiful. I heard it was Ryan and Dan's idea. I guess Dan's friend that did it is a Marine stationed in Kings Bay and he asked Mama for Sean's uniform so he could get it cleaned and done up. We didn't know it was for this. Krista was so touched." Ann sighed, enjoying the closeness of Dustin, the woody scent of his cologne filling her lungs.

They danced the night away, smiling and laughing as the crowd dwindled down. By the time Ann admitted her feet were hurting, it was nearly midnight and she was more than drunk on Jameson. Dustin laughed, offering to carry her up to her room for the night. Before Ann could protest, she was swept up into Dustin's arms, her arms looped around his neck, her head on his broad shoulder.

Mama and Daddy had already said their goodnight's long ago, leaving the younger crowd to celebrate. Krista and Ryan were the last to leave; sitting and watching the lingering partygoers finally leave. Ann and Dustin had wished Krista and Ryan the best before they too left. Krista had smiled that knowing smile at Ann, winking. Ann blushed again, knowing what Krista was referring to, a smile on her own face.

Ann giggled as Dustin crept up the stairs, quiet to not wake her parents. She felt like they were teenagers again, but only this time they were adults who knew what they were doing. Dustin toed open the door to Ann's bedroom, gently setting her onto unsteady feet. He made turn to leave; Ann put her hand on his arm, his darkened eyes questioning her.

"Help me out of this please." Ann motioned to the zipper in the back of the dress, her voice a whisper in the moonlight. Ann felt Dustin's hands on her back, pulling the zipper to her hips as the top of the dress pooled on her hipbones. Ann felt the rough callouses of Dustin's hands on her bare back, the softness of his lips on her shoulder. Ann moaned at the tenderness of it, the last time anyone had touched her like this was the last time she and Dustin had been in this same room so many years ago, before they broke up.

Ann turned in his arms, her eyes bright in the moonlight, her lips parted as Dustin touched his lips to hers. Ann felt the rush of heat pool in her pelvis, as she trembled at his touch. It had been too long for her since she had been touched.

Fallujah, Iraq

Logan took a deep breath at his computer desk, waiting for Skype to start up. He had emailed Ann back earlier in the day, and explained to Amy Kelly, the ombudsman, why Ann was his notification.

Mels was sitting on the edge of Logan's bed, watching the laptop screen intently. The call began to beep through, both of them knowing it was almost 11pm in Colorado. Jaye would be awake still, which Logan was sure of, she had always been a night owl as long as he knew her.

Jaye's bright blue eyes smiled when she saw Logan, it had been at the pre-deployment party since she last saw her "brother from another mother."

"Hey Logan, how are ya? Haven't heard from you in a while. What's up?" Jaye's voice sounded so happy to hear from him, Logan's gut twisted at what he was about to say.

Looking at the background behind Jaye, Logan realized she was at home. This didn't make what he had to say any better, but at least it wouldn't go farther than where it was.

"Jaye, I hate makin' this call to ya. But I promised Bonnie that if anything happened I'd make the call 'cause we all knew you'd rather hear it from me than not know at all with the way the regs are. Baby, I'm so sorry. We lost Bonnie on the way back from the Baharia project. The convoy hit an IED and the motherfuckers jumped us as we were scrambling to respond. I was the one who was with her when she passed, I did everything I could to help the Corpsman save her, but I just wasn't good enough. Bonnie did what we all knew she would, she ran out under fire to save our guys, and without her doing what she did, there'd be more guys going home with her. I'm so sorry Jaye, God I'm so sorry." Logan fought to get the words out before he broke down, he could hear Mels quietly sobbing behind him. Mels had been what was keeping him from going completely to pieces over the last few days since the attack.

The tears began to fall down Logan's cheeks as he watched the shocked look on Jaye's face turn to sobs. He never wanted to be the one to notify anyone, much less someone he considered family. Jaye would have never been told by the Navy with

Don't Ask, Don't Tell being in full effect. Bonnie's parents had already been notified as Bonnie was transported through Kuwait on the way to Dover, DE. Logan wasn't sure if they would notify Jaye or not, which was why he took it upon himself to Skype her.

Mels stepped up to the screen to offer her condolences to Jaye, telling her that she and Logan loved Jaye and would do anything they could to help. Bonnie was a close friend that many sought out to talk to more than they did medical treatment. She was a helluva Corpsman, and best friend. Mels knew Logan went to Bonnie when he couldn't talk to her about things, it was just natural.

Jaye thanked Mels through her tears as Mels disconnected the call. She turned Logan's desk chair around, tipping his head up to meet her teary green eyes. She could see that he was hurting; the death of Bonnie was finally reality for him. Mels had never seen Logan this utterly completely broken in all the years they had been together. She'd seen hurt in his eyes, but he was always one to keep his emotions under tight wraps.

"Come on, let's get you into bed. You've slept like shit for days, even with me here." Mels took Logan by the arm, hoisting him out of the chair. Logan shuffled over to the bed, crashing hard onto the light blue pillow. Mels stripped down to a pair of shorts, pulling Logan close to her, his skin warm against her chest. The sobs gradually subsided into sniffles, the sniffles into light snoring. Mels closed her eyes, knowing that rest was what they both needed to help deal with the loss of a close friend.

Mels woke in the darkness of Logan's quarters, the sheets of the bed kicked around their feet. She felt the comforting weight of Logan's body next to her, felt his fingertips on her skin. His fingers inched their way up her thigh, delving between her slick folds. Mels gasped when he crooked his fingers up towards her belly, his lips hot on her neck.

"Logan…" Mels gasped, pushing against his wrist, but he wasn't stopping. Mels felt him pull away from her neck, glancing over to see his eyes still closed, a serene look on his face. He was still asleep! The man was fucking her with his fingers in his sleep, which Mels knew he had done before. There had been plenty of times Mels and Logan had sex half asleep, and then wondered why they woke up spent and sore.

Mels pushed against Logan's chest, but he had her pinned with his body as his teeth bit into her nipple. Mels groaned, knowing that it was useless to fight against what was going on. Logan was bound and determined to finish, the needy weight on her body was clear.

"Mmh Ann…you feel so good baby girl." The groan of her name on his lips pushed Mels over the edge, her teeth sinking into his shoulder and nails clawing his back.

Logan's body went rigid, Mels wasn't sure if it was because of the pain she caused him, the orgasm he was shaking from or both. Either way he was alert and coherent, his eyes popping open as they darted over Mels' body.

"FUCK! Jesus, I'm sorry Mels. Jesus. Fuck!" Logan flopped back against the pillows, spent but emotionally frustrated. Waking up to Mels on his fingers and his shorts soaked in his own cum was not the plan of the day. Logan's face was red with embarrassment and shame for himself. He had been dreaming about being in the mountains in Colorado with Ann, making love to her. He was sure the dream was sparked by the very faint smell of her in his pillow that he hadn't noticed in his grief.

Mels wiped tears from her eyes, the shame and hurt evident in her eyes. Logan had gotten her off many times, but never had he done it while thinking she was another woman. Mels gathered up her clothes, dressing quickly. Logan watched her from the bed, apologizing vehemently.

The damage was done now, there wasn't any taking it back. Mels opened the door to his quarters, stepping out into the heat of the morning. The last thing she heard was Logan's bellowed "FUCK!" before the door clicked shut.

Chapter Twelve

An annoying tone broke the silence of the bedroom. Ann cracked an eye open, dawn was breaking, her bedroom was bathed in a soft orange glow. She rolled over onto her side, nearly falling from the full size bed onto the floor. Ann huffed, blindly reaching for the offending item making the noise, having half a mind to chuck it against the wall. She grumbled realizing that the unwelcome noise maker was her phone. Ann had missed a call (she wasn't sure how she missed the ringtone), with the email icon showing in the status bar. Who would be calling her during the night? Ann grumbled as she swiped her finger across the screen. The missed call notification popped up an 808 number, a quick google of the area code came up with Hawaii, Midway and Wake Islands.

Shaking her head to clear out the fog of sleep, Ann realized she didn't know anyone in those places. Whoever had called left a voicemail. The sleepy blonde smirked, why would someone she clearly doesn't know leave a voicemail? For the sake of comedic relief, she dialed into voicemail thinking it was probably someone drunk dialing. Static filled the beginning of the voicemail, Ann pulled the phone away from her ear, looking at the screen. The call was still going through, her fingers fumbled at the phone being in one hand. The solid weight fell on her chest as a voice came across the line, startling her.

"Hey Ann, umm... I thought I'd give you a call and see what you're up to. It's almost noon here and I'm on lunch. Shit, that means you're probably in bed asleep. Sorry. I hope you're okay. I emailed you back. If it's okay for me to call again, email me times that are good would ya? Ah, yeah would you just make sure they're in Mountain Standard Time, easier for me to remember with my watch being set to that time. Have a good night. Guess I'll talk to you later."

Ann scrambled for the phone, hitting save and replay. She hadn't really caught it on the first play; but on the second she realized the accent was heavy Georgian, and heard a plane flying overhead. Logan's voice sounded tired, but something else laced his words. It sounded like sadness, making Ann's good heart want to be able to reach out and touch him. Disappointment filled her, wishing she had been awake to answer his call. He sounded like he needed someone to talk to, and he was reaching out to her.

Exiting out of voicemail, Ann logged into her school email from her phone. Sure enough there was an email dated from four days ago, with Logan as the sender. Why would he be calling her and emailing her in the same week? There had to be some reason Logan was reaching out to her the way he was. Ann's curiosity got the best of her, her finger trembled as she clicked the subject line.

Ann,

Things ain't been the greatest over here, so I'm sorry I didn't reply to your email sooner. I've been working a bit since getting back from the project I was on, but it's hard to get into it. Sorry I didn't write you for almost a month, I was gone on a project and didn't have access to a computer or phone. Mail would have been a pain in the ass to get and get out. There will be times I get pulled out to a project and communication will be pretty silent for the time I'm there. I promise as soon as I can when I get back from stuff like that I'll try to get in touch with you. That's the shit part about being at war, contact can be hit or miss.

I'm thinking you're right. If things work out between us while I'm gone, we should take that horseback getaway up to Pike's Peak. I need some down time after this deployment, and being out there in the mountains camping with you sounds like the best idea in the world. We'll fish, I'll hunt and do some riding. I want you to see my world and have a break from that big city you live in. I couldn't deal with that city life, I hate going into the Springs for work enough as it is. If you fly out, I'd pick you up in Colorado Springs, that's the closest airport to the house in Cascade. It might be a bit expensive though, so if you need to save money fly into Denver. It's a bit of a drive, but I'd do it for you. You'll love Colorado, it's so different from Georgia.

Thanks for making me feel better about college. I'll think about it, it's not a huge priority for me right now. You're going to have $100k wrapped up in med school? Shit! I wasn't aware it cost that much, damn! But I guess learning to be a doctor can't be cheap, especially when you make so much money later on. You'll get it paid off and then you'll be okay, I'm sure of that.

Sorry to hear about your Daddy and what he went through with his wife and jail. Butch ends up in jail a good bit for different things, and we'll just leave that there. I've learned to live without him in my life.

Yeah, I have a roommate at the house in Colorado, her name is Melanie Heiderschiedt. She's from Minnesota. I call her Mels or H-12. She's a CM like me as well, and we are deployed together. She's probably my best friend outside our Corpsman Chief Bonnie Tate. When I can't talk to Mels, I go to Bonnie and vice versa. They are exceptional women that I am proud to call friend.

Speaking of Bonnie, I need to get something off my chest. When we were coming back from the project, the convoy hit an IED and the ragheads jumped us. Bonnie rushed out to do her job and start treating the wounded. I saw her take some fire, but she seemed okay and kept working on our guys. When things seemed safe I ran over to check on her and saw she was seriously wounded. One of her Corpsmen and me did all we could to stop the blood loss, even with Bonnie trying to direct us. I think she knew anyway, and was still determined to help the wounded. If it hadn't been for her more guys wouldn't have survived the attack. Bonnie died in my arms out on that road. I promised her I would call her wife and notify her since the Navy won't due to DADT. To be honest with you, I'm not looking forward to making that Skype call to Jaye. It will kill us both, and I don't know what to say. But, I'm a man of my word and I'm not gonna deny Jaye knowing, and its better it came from a friend than someone she doesn't know. I emailed the ombudsman, Amy Kelly, and made you my notification. I know it says a lot, but I just don't want you going like Jaye and maybe not having someone to call you in case something bad happens to me. Not saying it will or won't, 'cause I can't make you a promise like that. I'm just saying I did it, so someone will let you know.

Don't worry about sending me anything all the time. Just whenever, I'm not expecting much really. I know you got things you got to do, and a life over there. I'll still be here a bit longer. I hope your sister's wedding was nice, yeah, if I'd been home I would have been happy to escort you in my uniform. I'm sure you looked beautiful in your dress.

I'm surprised you didn't know about the pillowcase. Either way it's been a welcome source of comfort. Kinda like you're here with me in bed, and I don't mean that in a sexual way. I don't know how to fucking explain it without it coming off dirty. Just know it's not in a dirty way that I think about you. I don't see the night stars much, as I usually at work. But sometimes I catch myself glancing at my watch and my mind wanders to what you could be doing at that time over there. There's a seven hour time difference between us I think, so I get confused on time a lot between us.

I can call and Skype from here, but that seven hour time difference I just mentioned can be a problem. Just let me know what times work for you on MST and maybe I can call ya sometime? As far as Skype, I'll have to add you to my contacts list and if I see you on when I can be on, we can try that too. It makes me feel good that my emails make you feel better, I know how lonely it can be, being the one left at home.

You are beautiful Ann, and 26 is a good age. No, I'm not 29. I'm actually 32.

Well darlin', guys aren't that great at thinking about themselves as being good looking. Kinda comes off a little unmanly ya know? Don't have a wife, or an ex-wife. Never been married. Had a couple of ex-girlfriends though, but everyone has ex's right?

I heard rumor they are bringing in a CMC from a reserve battalion to take over for the night Chief so I can go back on days. He's supposed to be showing up soon, and I hope to hell he's better than the one he's replacing.

Since I didn't have a way to contact you while I was on the project, Bonnie suggested I sit down with a notebook and write you. And it helped me to get some of these thoughts and feelings out on paper. I know you care about me in some way, it's apparent in your emails and letters. If you didn't want me knowing what you looked like, you never would have sent that picture I have taped up on my desk. I glance up at it often when I'm writing you emails, and the image stayed with me when I was gone. I know how hard it can be to put feelings into words and make them make sense. Hell, I can't fucking put most of what I think into spoken words, but I can write it down. You'll realize it once we start talking, you'll probably beg for me to start emailing and writing you again.

Ann, I know I'm asking a lot of you darlin' but with everything that's gone on lately, and the way I feel and the way you seem to feel I think I got rights to ask you this. Would ya consider trying this whole dating thing between us while I'm gone? It won't be much different than what we are doing now, except that we're exclusive to each other? I promise when I get back I'll make it all up to you if we can make this stand through the next few months. If you say no, I totally understand, and I hope we could still be friends. Let me know.

I gotta get going into work, got to do some paperwork concerning Bonnie. I'm gonna miss her; she was a helluva Doc and friend. Take care of you Ann, and know you're not far from my thoughts.

Logan

Ann couldn't hold back the tears falling down her face, she tried to force herself to choke back the sobs threatening to fill the bedroom. Logan had been in an attack, and he had lost his best friend. Ann grieved for him, she had no idea what it was like to lose someone like that. Sure she had family members die, but never in front of her eyes.

Ann felt a hand glide up her thigh as a groan sounded from the warm body next to her. Dustin's eyes focused on Ann's face, concern evident in his face as he rolled over to face Ann.

"Ann? You alright babe? What's wrong?" His voice showed every bit of care for the woman he was in love with. Dustin always hated seeing Ann cry, he couldn't get the sinking feeling out of his gut that he was the reason she was crying now. Last night wasn't a mistake, it was sudden and unexpected. He knew it wasn't in his plans to wake up in Ann's bed this morning. He was sure his Grandma was wondering why he didn't come home last night from the wedding. Dustin didn't regret last night, until he saw the tears in Ann's eyes.

Ann clutched her cellphone like it was the only lifeline she had to the world. Dustin gave her a puzzled look as she glanced at him and the door to her bedroom. Thoughts flitted through her mind about Logan and what he asked of her, guilt sitting in her gut like a greasy meal from a truck stop dive. She hated how she felt at the moment, torn between someone she knew intimately and someone she was just beginning to understand.

"Dustin, you gotta leave. I'm sorry." Ann pulled the sheet up around her chest, her knees holding the sheet in place. Tears slipped down her cheeks, she didn't even bother wiping them away.

Dustin sighed, he pulled his hand back from reaching out for Ann. He knew her well enough that it was in his best interest to leave. Dustin reached for his clothes, dressing quickly before pulling on his boots. He grabbed his hat off the free standing mirror, wringing the brim in his hands as he bent down to brush Ann's cheek with his lips. She jerked away from him like he was a hot iron. Dustin sighed, shaking his head heading for the bedroom door.

Ann heard Dustin going down the old wood stairs, along with the short exchange between him and her father in the kitchen. It wasn't until she heard the screen door slam and his rental car leave that she cried in earnest. Why did things have to be so confusing and heartbreaking?

Chapter Thirteen

Logan peered across the shop at the new night Chief. Word on the street was he came from a Reserve battalion out of Chicago and this was his third desert deployment in three years. That alone made Logan respect the hell out of the guy, someone dedicated enough to do three deployments to hell nearly back to back. Dedicated or crazy, probably both the way Logan saw him grinning and laughing with Mels and the other guys in the shop. Logan turned back to the MRAP he was working on, it needed an oil change for the crew that was taking it out in the morning. Oil and grease up to his elbows, Logan turned when a thick Irish accent addressed him.

"Hey brother, how you doing on that oil change?" The bright blue eyes and boyish grin made Logan grin in return. Logan clasped the hand sticking out roughly, not caring he was getting the Chief's hand dirty. The man clearly didn't care, still grinning as he squeezed Logan's hand in his.

"Going good. Heard you're the new Chief for nights?" Logan sized the guy up, he seemed to be about the same age and size as Logan was. He might look the pretty boy, but his hands told a different story.

"Aye, I'm Stephens replacement. Name's Padraic Flannery. Ye can call me Paddy. Damn nice ta meet 'cha. What's yer name?" Logan understood the Irish accent easily, his Grandmother came straight from Ireland during the War.

"Logan Dixon. Nice to meet ya Paddy. Where ya from?" Logan hated small talk, but he knew it was best that he got to know the Chief he would be working with.

"Chicago. Volunteered for this deployment when I got the call about it. Don't got no one to keep me back in the States so why not make meself useful?"

The grin on Paddy's face was infectious. "Where're ye from Dixon?"

"Colorado by way of Georgia. I'll see about getting you squared away tonight if that's good with you?" Logan needed to get the MRAP moving, and this little chit chat was cutting into his personal time table.

"Aye. Heiderschiedt offered to get me around today. If you want to lag back a bit and help tonight that'd be grand as well." Flannery clapped Logan on the shoulder before turning to walk away.

So Mels was offering to get a Chief acclimated? That was a new one for Logan, even when she came onto 17 she hated the Chief's being around her. She had latched onto Logan pretty quick with him being a First Class like her at that time. Logan smirked to himself, whatever floated Mels' boat. They hadn't talked much since the incident in his quarters, the only time they talked was when work required it.

Logan finished up the oil change on the MRAP, hollering for Johnson to run it out to the yard. Looking across the shop, Logan saw Mels and Chief Flannery talking animatedly. Mels was laughing out loud at a joke Flannery had told, the shit eating grin on his face told it all.

Logan hung back after his work day was over, just as Flannery asked to help him get acclimated. Flannery followed Logan around the shop, getting the run down on what work the equipment in the shop was needing to go out. Logan introduced each of the night mechanics to Flannery before he did his introduction brief. Scanning the group of mechanics, Logan noticed Mels missing. He thought it odd that she wasn't there, seeing how earlier she was cozied up with the Irishman. Excusing himself from the brief, Logan headed off for the galley and his quarters.

Logan cussed to himself when he realized the galley was closed, and wouldn't be open again for another two hours. He headed over to the shop, snagging an MRE out of the case in the office. They weren't the most tasty thing to eat, but would do in a pinch, especially since Logan was ready for a shower and bed. He had to get up early, and with staying late to help Flannery, time was passing quickly.

Punching in the code for his door, Logan's eyes adjusted to the change of brightness to dim. He was shocked to find Mels sitting at his desk, using his computer. That wasn't someone he thought to find in his quarters with the way things had been between them as of late.

"Mels what are you doing here?" Logan gruffed closing the door behind him.

Mels' green eyes looked up at Logan, her eyes looked puffy and red. His anger immediately flared, whoever made Mels cry was going to get an ass kicking from him when they tracked the fucker down.

"I came to talk to you." Mels took a deep breath as she stood up from the desk, walking slowly towards Logan. Her breath hitched in her throat when she saw the anger burning in his eyes, he'd seen the hurt in her eyes. She knew she couldn't hide from him for long, he knew her better than anyone.

"Who's made you cry Mels? I swear I'll hunt his ass down and kick it from here to BIAP." Logan's eyes cut sharp on Mels' eyes, waiting for the answer. His body was rigid, fighting to keep his anger locked down, his breathing steady as she walked up into his personal space.

Mels reached out to lay her fingers against his cheek, her eyes connecting with his. He heard the sigh she tried to stifle, seeing her body relax as her emotions surged. Mels wasn't one to break down in front of just anyone, Logan was the only one she trusted with her emotions. Mels' lips parted to breathe the name that hung up on her tongue. She bit her top lip between her teeth nervously, her eyes started to water.

Logan's eyes snapped shut when he realized what she wasn't saying. A hand nervously pushed his cover up farther on his head, as he blew out a breath. "Fuck Mels. I'm sorry. Things have been so fucked up since Baharia. And Bonnie and Jaye. And I'm sorry for what happened that morning. It wasn't like I meant it to."

Mels bit her lips together, gathering the courage to respond, Logan was never one to say he was sorry. This was a big step for him, admitting regrets and weakness. He was her strength when she was weak, and now that strength was fading. The tears threatened to fall as Mels pulled a piece of folded paper out of her back pocket, handing it to Logan.

The piece of paper hung in the air between them, Logan looking at it inquisitively. "What's this Mels?" Logan unfolded the paper, knowing exactly what it was when he saw the name in the top box written in Mels' neat script. Reading through the boxes, Logan's gut clenched as his heart stopped. "Why honey? You're the best damn mechanic I got! I ain't gonna sign this."

Mels sighed, forcing her emotions into check to convince Logan this was what she needed. "Logan, I need this request signed by you and approved up the chain. It's what I got to do for me. Please sign it."

"I ain't signing it woman. I'm not losing you. I need you here working." Logan threw the request on his desk with the MRE, turning to look at Mels.

Mels stood in the middle of the small room, her body language telling Logan she was pissed and hurt. "Logan, please. I need to leave the battalion. I'll have all my stuff out of the house before you get back. It's something I need to do. Johnson can step up for me. You've got Flannery now too."

"Tell me why. It ain't like you to up and fucking do something like this without a damn good reason. If it's about what happened the morning after the Skype call with Jaye, I told ya I'm sorry. I ain't a mind reader Mels, you gotta throw me a bone here." Logan splayed his hands, confused as to why this was happening.

"It's more than just what happened in here Logan. We've been dancing since Apra Harbor, and it hasn't stopped, even after what happened. I stayed even after we spilt bedrooms because I knew you needed me to help pay the bills. I knew you needed my shoulder when all those whores walked out of your bedroom. I was proud as hell when you got tapped for your anchor, knowing I'd never get mine. When Adam did what he did to me, you were there for me. I can't ever tell you how much that means to me that you were there. But, I know now that you don't need me anymore, as much as you may think you do. It's time for me to move on with my life." Mels sniffled, struggling at keeping the tears at bay.

"Why don't you tell me what happened after Apra Harbor that you kicked me out of your bed? I walked through all those whores because I was still in love with ya! I couldn't find you in any of them! And when Adam raped you and left you to die I did what I had to. I did what was right for you! I do need you Melanie; I need you here to keep me together. I'm a fuckin' mess with Bonnie gone, the attack and telling Jaye. I needed you those days, I still need you." Logan was losing grip on his emotions, his breath was ragged as his voice broke.

Mels began to cry, hot tears fell onto the chest of her uniform t-shirt, and she hated crying in front of him. "You want to know what happened after Apra that I kicked you out of my bed? You think you're ready for something like that Logan? You don't need me Logan, your heart is where it needs to be--with Ann. I'm not mad about her, I'm actually really happy for you. She's what I can't ever be for you, and as much as you try to hide it, it's written all over your fucking face. Dreamers never lie, and you had her name on your lips when you made me cum. It should have been her with you instead of me. It's what your heart wants and where it belongs!" Mels began to shake as her emotions raged through her drained body. The attack on the convoy scared the hell out of her, she was afraid that it would be her that would be notifying Ann of Logan being killed or injured. Mels grieved along with Logan for the loss of Bonnie and the notification of Jaye; it was a hard hit to her system.

"Melanie, what happened after Apra? You gotta tell me, I gotta know why we went from lovers to friends. I made it clear to Ann in my last email I wanted to try dating her, but she ain't replied to me yet." Logan could feel his heart ache for Mels, knowing what she was saying was true. Mels hadn't picked on him about Ann as she had all the other women he dated, which was the telltale sign that Mels liked Ann. Mels had come to get a transfer request signed, not hash out everything between them.

"Logan, I lost our baby after Apra. I was three months along and had a miscarriage while I was home on leave in Minnesota. Had to have surgery." Mels watched as Logan's jaw fell open, his body sinking into the desk chair. She hadn't ever wanted him to know, Mels dealt with that joy and pain alone. Logan wasn't ready to be a parent and neither was she at that point. They were friends that ended up in bed together for a long last night of a deployment. It wasn't meant to be, not then, not now.

Logan struggled to breathe, feeling the world start to spin around him. Mels had been pregnant with his baby, and yet she didn't tell him. The loss of their baby was the reason why everything changed between them. He understood now why everything was the way it had been, she was masking her pain being around him.

"I wish you woulda told me you were pregnant. I woulda done the right thing and married you." The words came out a whisper Mels barely heard.

"Logan, we both know that would have never worked out. As much as you love me, you need to let me go." The words were the truth, she knew they never would have been able to be a couple in the usual sense of the word, and she knew it was time for her to go.

Logan looked at the request on his desk, grabbing the pen off his desk. He checked the box for approval and signed his name and rank in the appropriate box. Mels was right, they never would have worked out as married with a baby. Even if he thought it was the right thing to do.

Logan handed the request to Mels, seeing the half smile on her face trembling. He heard the door click shut behind her before his face fell into his hands. Logan's world was crumbling around him, sobs wracking his shoulders as the pain bubbled to the surface and consumed him.

Chapter Fourteen

Ann heard her text message alert pinging in the front seat as she loaded up her bags to head back to New York. Spring break was over, the wedding was beautiful and it was time to go back to the security of her normal life of school. Last night with Dustin wasn't a mistake, but waking up next to him after reading Logan's email was. It took everything within Ann to not start screaming at Dustin when she told him he needed to leave. Her heart was beating so fast in her chest she thought it was going to explode. Logan had been in an attack, had his best friend die in his arms and still had to notify the spouse.

Ann couldn't imagine the pain he was going through thousands of miles away. She spent an hour that morning at her mother's computer emailing Logan back, the words came from her heart through her fingers. Even though she was half a world away, Ann hoped that her words would bring Logan some comfort.

Ann said her goodbyes to her family, reaching into her purse to answer the text that wouldn't leave her alone.

Meet me at Bertie's for lunch please?

Ann sighed, she at least owed Dustin an explanation for her abrupt behavior earlier in the morning. Her fingers slid across the keys, the response short and sweet. Stashing the phone back into her purse, Ann headed out the driveway and into Hazlehurst for lunch with Dustin.

On the drive into town, scattered thoughts floated around in Ann's head about what she would say to Dustin. He was sure to be confused with how they danced the night away during the reception, ended up in bed together that night, and then Ann asking him to leave with tears in her eyes the next morning. If the tables were turned, Ann was sure she would feel like crap and want an explanation too. She and Dustin weren't kids anymore; they were adults now, consenting adults, who had stronger feelings than kids did.

Ann pulled into a parking space on the street outside the small, family owned diner. When Ann was in high school she used to wait tables at Bertie's, it was her first job and the one she kept until she left for medical school. Stepping through the glass door was like stepping back in time, nothing had really changed in the diner and it still smelled of Bertie's homemade peach pies.

"ANNANY STRANAHAN!" A woman's gleeful voice hollered across the diner, making Ann's head snap to the left. A slight woman with white hair and thick glasses walked over; wrapping Ann in a tight hug, making the younger woman blush.

"Child, it's been a long time since you've been in here. I think the last time was the last day you worked for me. How are you dear? I heard your sister's a kept woman now." Bertie smiled brightly at

Ann, no one could ever not smile back at Bertie Smith.

"I'm good Bertie. Going to medical school in New York. Yeah Krista got married yesterday, it was a beautiful wedding. Looks like you're doing well here." Ann glanced to the men sitting at the counter, not seeing Dustin.

"Oh I can't complain dear, the farmers and their coffee in the morning keep me going," Bertie leaned in close, whispering so only Ann could hear. "I see your young man Dustin is sitting over at table seven by himself. I'm guessing he's waiting on you? He's grown up into a strapping young man." Bertie winked as she elbowed Ann gently, the blush rising up once more.

"Thanks Bertie. Yeah I think he's waiting for me." Ann hugged the grandmotherly owner once more before walking over to table seven. Dustin looked up from his menu, his slight grin making Ann smile.

"Thanks for meeting me Ann, please have a seat." Dustin motioned to the chair across from him, knowing Ann wouldn't be comfortable sitting in the chair next to him. His hat sat brim up in the chair, as Ann set her purse down in the chair next to her.

Ann smoothed her dress over the backs of her thighs as she sat down, unaware she was holding her breath as her eyes met Dustin's. He had such kind and caring eyes that was one thing Ann always loved about him. Ann picked up the menu, knowing that she wasn't really hungry but needed to eat before she got on the road. The waitress came over and took their orders, Ann was not surprised that Dustin ordered a bacon cheeseburger, that man loved his beef. Ann ordered a salad and sweet tea, she didn't want anything heavy with how her stomach was feeling.

"So, Ann, was what up with this morning? I didn't regret last night one bit, until you kicked me out this morning. Even your Daddy gave me a funny look as I passed him in the kitchen going out the front door. I'm really confused." Dustin's deep voice softened, trying to ply Ann to explain things. She was the only one who had answers for the teary goodbye in her bedroom. Dustin was willing to talk it through and do what he had to, to fix whatever was wrong. He loved Ann that much still, after all these years that passed between them.

Ann took a deep drink of the sweet tea in front of her, the ice tinkling against the glass. She didn't know how to go about telling Dustin about Logan, without coming off like she had used him. Ann wasn't one of those kind of girls, the last person she had done anything with had been Dustin himself when he was home one summer from college in Montana. That was a long time ago, and they had fumbled through it, Ann embarrassed thoroughly when it was over.

"Dustin, I'm sorry about this morning. I was really emotional with everything going on lately. I guess I should tell you the truth, since it's the only thing I know right now. See, there's this guy that's over in Iraq right now that I've been corresponding with since December. And he called me sometime last night and left me a message, I wouldn't figure he would call unless it was something important. His name is Logan and he's a Chief with the Navy Seabees. And he said he left me an email, I read that email. He lost his best friend in a roadside bombing they were in. She died in his arms. All through that pain he asked me if I'd consider dating him, seeing if something could come out of all of this. That was why I was crying." Ann felt better getting the truth out, as much as she knew it was killing Dustin inside. She watched his face for any sign of emotion, hoping he would get pissed off. Something was better than nothing.

Dustin ran his long finger over the condensation beading on the glass in front of him. What had he expected being gone for so long? Ann to just fall in his lap like old times? It had been almost four years since had last seen her that first summer between semesters. Blowing out a breath,

Dustin looked over at the tears welling in Ann's bright blue eyes. He always hated seeing her cry, he felt like he had to protect her from the world ever since they were teenagers.

"Honey, I wish you'd told me about this yesterday, last night wouldn'ta happened. I'm not gonna sit here and be the other man, especially for a guy who puts his ass on the line over there. I guess last night was just you getting me out of your system then huh? I've always had feelings for you Ann, even when we weren't together. Probably because you're the first girl I ever was with and the only one I wanted for so long. If you want to be with this guy, I'll step out. I got too much respect for those guys over there to be an asshole and be the other man." Dustin pushed his chair back carefully, laying a $50 out on the table from his hip pocket. He picked up his hat, curling the brim in his hand.

"I'll see ya around Ann, lunch is on me." Dustin drawled before placing his hand on Ann's shoulder. "Tell Logan I said thanks for his service."

Ann sniffled and nodded; watching Dustin walk out of the diner, stopping at the door to look back at Ann once more. A small smile turned up one corner of his mouth as he clamped his hat on, before disappearing out the door.

The waitress brought out both of their meals, Ann told her to give them to someone else that was waiting on lunch and to keep the change from the tab. She knew that waitress was getting an almost $30 tip. Ann grabbed her purse and headed out to her truck before the tears fell. She knew Dustin would do what was right, she just never thought he would be so accepting about it. She expected him to get angry, say something mean or yell. He didn't do any of those things, and that was what hurt the worst.

Sitting in her truck, Ann took a deep breath. She almost wanted to chase after Dustin and tell him it wasn't like he was the other man, but in her heart of hearts that would have been a lie. Sleeping with Dustin hadn't been her getting him out of her system, sleeping with him had been two lonely people finding solace in each other. Ann linked up the Bluetooth to her phone, plugging the phone into charge. She needed to get on the road, it was a long drive up to New York. She could always pick up something to eat on the road as her stomach rumbled; reminding her she'd now skipped out on two meals.

Ann felt better after stopping in Emporia, VA to get some dinner. The double bacon cheeseburger and fries had never tasted as good as they had that night. Ann even splurged and mowed through a piece of strawberry cheesecake. Thank God for small favors that the hotel had a restaurant in the lobby. Ann didn't make it as far as she usually did on the first day driving back from Georgia, but she chalked that up to the emotional morning and lunch before she left Hazlehurst.

The hotel room was cool and dark, all Ann could think about was sleeping. Well, a hot shower and sleep. Turning on the shower tap, Ann let her fingers dance through the warming water. A shower always made her feel better when she felt crappy, and right now her emotions were raw. The hot water felt so good rushing over her weary skin, Ann savored the quiet time, letting her mind wander.

Towel wrapped around her wet hair, Ann propped herself up in bed to flip through the channels on TV. She purposely skipped anything that remotely looked like news, settling on a movie with her favorite male lead, Channing Tatum, called Dear John. It was about halfway through the movie, as John is reading a letter from Savannah that Ann saw the parallelisms between her and Logan. While she hadn't met Logan in person, the similarities were there nonetheless.

Ann was transfixed watching the entire movie, tears flowing freely down her cheeks. Why did she let a movie get to her so deep? Probably because the movie was what she was going through at the moment, she could empathize with Savannah and her feelings while John was deployed. So many emotions, so many moments of silence, so many unknown things. Ann reached over to set an alarm on her phone, seeing she missed a call while she was in the shower. Pulling up the call log, she realized it was that 808 number again. Her heart beat quickly in her chest as she dialed into her voicemail. She'd missed a call from Logan again, and he'd left her a message. Static filled the line before his voice came through, making Ann click on the speaker phone. She clutched the phone in her hands, as he eyes closed, imagining him standing with a phone in his hand talking to her.

"Hey Ann, I know it's late over there, but I thought I'd give a call and see if I could get in touch with you. Umm, I guess if I ain't got a choice I'll talk to your voicemail. I'm just getting around to head into work. I hope you're back in New York safe and sound. I worry about you when you're driving by yourself like that. I'm doing ok over here, doing the best I can.

Don't worry about me you hear? I'll check my email for you when I get off work. Just wanted you to know you're in my thoughts. Take care of you. Gotta go."

The voicemail ended, Ann clicked the save button before setting the alarm on her phone. Turning off the lights, she pulled an extra pillow into her arms, wrapping her body around it. Logan sounded a little better than he did in the voicemail from the morning, but it still made Ann worry about him. Until he was home with her, she would worry about him. That was what you did with someone you loved, you worried and cared. Even with Logan half a world away, Ann couldn't help her feelings for him.

Chapter Fifteen

"Ye looking rough brother. Did ye not sleep last night?" Paddy's strong voice made Logan turn his head to see his counterpart standing next to the desk that Logan was logging his work into, holding a coffee cup.

"Please tell me you ain't another one of those coffee swilling fat asses who never work?" Logan needed someone who played ball, not someone who doubled the work for him later. That was what Logan had hated about Stephens, and with losing Mels, the work would be deeper than usual if Flannery didn't play ball.

Paddy guffawed, handing the cup to Logan. "Ye look like ye need it more'n me. Here, have a swig." Logan took the proffered mug, taking a long drink. He sputtered and coughed as Flannery pounded on Logan's back. The coffee burned all the way down, but not just from the heat. The Irishman drank loaded coffee, and how he got it through the airport Logan wasn't sure.

"I'll be goddamned Paddy! How the hell did you get it through the airport?" Logan choked as the fire burned in his throat, seizing his lungs.

"Lord's name brother! When there's a will there's a way. I can make ye one in the morning when we swap shifts. How about this weekend we get the boys together for some rugby? I heard ye play." Paddy's boyish grin made Logan snicker out loud, this was a guy he knew he could get along with.

"Yeah, I'd go for one of them in the morning. Some rugby sounds good, haven't played since before Heiderschiedt busted her finger trying to hook me." Logan's grin faded at the off handed mention of his now gone best friend. Logan had watched her leave on the convoy going down to Kuwait, unable to even say goodbye. The last he saw of her was her trademark smirk as her eyes met his, before she slung up into the MTVR.

"Ah the elusive Melanie H-12. Aye, she was a beauty. Certainly full of fire. She came to me a couple of nights ago asking me to sign her transfer request back stateside. I asked her why she didn't go to ye to get it signed. She said it was complicated with tears in her eyes. I hated sending her off to ye, but regs are regs. I take it ye signed it then?" Paddy took a drink of the mug, his face twisting up at the burn of coffee in his throat.

"Yeah, I did what I had to do. Did what was right. Hated to see her go, but it was for the best. I'm sure whatever battalion she lands at will be glad to have her. And before you ask, I ain't fucking talking about why it was complicated." Logan put up that wall, not only to protect his anchor, but to protect his heart.

"I understand ye. Sometimes when we're gone to places like this too long with the same people the lines 'tween professional and personal blur. I had a deployment wife once. Sweetest girl when we were out, but when we were back in port she wouldn'ta give me the time of day. That's just how it goes. Yer still alright with me Dixon. Get on outta here and get some chow and rack time. I got it." Logan visibly deflated at the older Chief's observation, and his willingness to keep things quiet between them.

"Alright. I'm done here, fuckin' going to bed." Logan bumped fists with Flannery before putting his cover and Oakley's on. The moon dust was kicking up something terrible, so Logan grabbed an MRE out of the office again before heading for his quarters. The dust bit at his bare arms and hands, the keffiyeh tight around his face and neck. Fighting the sand wasn't anything fun, it was small, abrasive and got into everything. Logan had to be sure to check his weapon every time before they went out, and keep his Oakley's handy.

Stripping down to just his pants and bare feet, Logan powered up his laptop.

He was sure there was an email in there from Ann, it had been a few days since he emailed her back and called her twice. Both times he got her voicemail; but just hearing her voice in his ear, even a recorded message, made him perk up a bit.

Opening his inbox there was an email from Ann in response to his email. While he knew it would be hit or miss on them catching each other on the phone that was always going to be the problem with him being seven hours ahead and half a world away. At least they still had mail and email, that wasn't something that could be as easily missed as a phone call.

Logan,

It makes me feel better to hear that you're okay. Going without hearing from you for a month scared the hell out of me. If you can please let me know when you're going out on a project so I don't worry as much about you. I know there is only so much you can say without getting in trouble, but if you can please let me know?

I want to go with you out to Pike's Peak. Even if things don't work out between us while you're deployed, we can always try again when you are physically in the states. I can only imagine that you would want time away from the world being stuck where you are. I want to spend that time with you. I'll have to see where the flights are cheapest into, and when you're coming home before I make any concrete plans.

I didn't realize your roommate was a woman. I'm glad that you have friends like that you can trust. I'm so sorry to hear about Bonnie, I can't imagine how that feels for you losing a friend like that and being under attack. It makes me worry even more for you, and I hope that you were able to find the words to bring her wife some comfort. If I were in her shoes, I would rather hear it from a friend than a stranger. I'm glad you put me on the notification list for you; I couldn't bear not

*knowing something had happened to you.
I think it would break my heart.*

*Krista's wedding was beautiful, I'll
try and gets some pictures sent off to you
somehow, either physical or email when
they come back from the photographer. I
have plans once I get back to NY to send
you some more cookies. I'm at my
parents' house now, packing up to leave. I
should be back to my apartment sometime
tomorrow evening. Probably by the time
you get this I'll be back in NY.*

*I hope you've been cuddled up with
my pillow. I know you don't mean
anything dirty by it, I just hope it's
brought you some comfort during these
tough times. I wish I could be there to
hold you and remind you that someone
over here loves and worries about you. I
think of you often, as crazy as that may
sound, but it makes me feel better when I
feel lonely to know you're probably
thinking of me too.*

Anytime between 4pm and 10pm Colorado time I can be on Skype. Anytime between 4pm and 3am Colorado time you can call and get ahold of me. I don't care if you wake me up, it's you and I know you need to talk. I want to hear your voice and want to talk to you. I want to make this work between us.

I don't care that you're 32, age is only a number. My parents have almost ten years between them, and they're amazing together. You're a very good looking man Logan, I was surprised when you said you were never married. Everyone has exes, even me, although I only have one ex. Long story.

I hope the replacement CMC is better than the last one you had, maybe he will keep things running better so you don't have to work so hard?

I do care about you Logan; I could even go as far as saying that I'm falling in love with you. I know, another crazy thought, but between all these emails, and letters, and the phone calls, I can tell you have feelings for me just like I do for you. Back during WWII that's how people fell in love, through letters, this isn't much different. I want to try this dating thing with you. So yes, let's be exclusive and try, I want to be there in Colorado for you when you get home. I want to be the girl on your arm at all those functions for the Navy and have you be there for me at my graduation from medical school.

I need to get on the road Logan, I hope this email makes you feel better about things. You're always in my thoughts and prayers, take care of you for me.

Love,

Ann

Logan fired up Skype, adding Ann's Skype username to his contact list. It showed her offline, but that was okay, it was only 5pm in Colorado, and she was probably still traveling back from Georgia.

He hated the thought of her driving back and forth by herself, even though she probably knew the route by heart. He would stay logged in, maybe she would log in when she got home?

He tore into the MRE, forcing the pretty much tasteless food down with a Galorade and a bottle of water. Ann admitted having feelings for him, admitting being in love with him. That was something that took him by surprise somewhat, although he had a thought it was coming. Logan wasn't the best at putting his feelings out there, but Ann had been smart enough to read between the lines and catch his drift. That made him feel better that they were on the same page, it made things much simpler.

Digging through his footlocker, Logan found one of the better brown uniform t-shirts in his collection. He dug through the bottom of his footlocker, finding his spare pair of dog tags and a fouled anchor Navy Cross pendant that the chaplain had given him when they landed in Kuwait. Logan strung the pendant onto the chain with the dog tags, wrapping them up in the folded t-shirt. Grabbing a sheet of paper out of his notebook, he scribbled a note to Ann to go with the items he packed into a small box. A little bit of high pressure tape and a Sharpie and the box was ready to run to the base post office in the morning. He had a tangible reminder of Ann on his bed, it was only fair in his mind that she had something of his to hold onto when the nights got a bit more than lonely.

Logan dialed into Ann's cellphone through Skype, adding it onto her Skype info. It didn't ring before going into her voicemail, which meant the phone was either dead or turned off. The thought of her phone off made him worried, knowing he couldn't do anything from half a world away. Logan sighed, finishing stripping out of his uniform. The shower sounded like a great idea at the moment, even if the water was tepid at best. That was one thing he was looking forward to when he got back to the states, a real bed, a real meal and a really hot shower. If he could wrangle it around to work out right, he'd book a hotel for the weekend he pulled in, make sure Ann was there to meet him on the flight line and take her out to a nice dinner after he got a shower. That would be how he would want to spend his first real date with Ann, dinner at a nice restaurant in Cali, an expensive hotel room on the beach and just the two of them together for the weekend.

The water and soap felt good against his weary skin, Logan sucked some of the water into his mouth, swishing it around and spitting it against the wall of the shower. Turning off the water, Logan was busy sluicing the water off his dripping body, when he heard the unmistakable tone of a Skype call coming through. Stepping over to his desk, he grabbed the towel off the back of the chair and wrapped it around his waist before sitting down.

His heart thudded in his chest when he saw the icon and name flashing in the top right corner of his screen—Ann.

Chapter Sixteen

Ann was tired and stressed from the drive home from Virginia. She hated DC traffic and the traffic around the City was even worse. By the time she got her bags in the door, the sole thought on her mind was a shower and a drink. Passing by her computer on the last trip out to the truck, Ann powered it on. She was hoping that maybe Logan had emailed her back, and that he was thinking along the same lines she was concerning this relationship they were trying to build. There wasn't any harm in trying, the worst that could happen was that they wouldn't work out while he was gone, and they could always try again when he got back.

Ann stripped out of her clothes, leaving a trail between her bedroom and bathroom. The hot water surging over her skin made her cry out, every nerve ending was firing inside her body. She was still emotional from the meeting with Dustin, and Logan's email. Anyone who wouldn't be emotional after all of that had something wrong with them. Ann ran a towel through her wet hair, walking past her computer to make a Jameson and Coke. She heard a bloop sound, looking over at her computer, someone had added her to their Skype contact list. Ann finished making her drink, plopping down into the computer chair with a towel wrapped around her head. She was tired, the dark spots under her eyes were apparent with her makeup washed off.

Looking up at the notification window she saw the user name as 'SeabeeCMDixon', Ann's heart started beating quickly, her palms got sweaty as she clicked the button to accept the request. When she heard the tones of the call going through did she realize she clicked 'accept & call'. Part of her hoped he was there, he had just added her within the last thirty minutes, why wouldn't he be there? Another part of her that was nervous as hell hoped he wasn't there, she didn't know what to say to him. The call connected, and Ann saw him for the first time with her own eyes.

Her breath caught in her throat; his hair was damp and he was shirtless. Scars of varying length, width and depth crisscrossed what she could see of his tanned chest. A tattoo covered part of his chest high on the right. His cobalt blue eyes trained on her, his gaze pierced right through her. Ann could see his breath hitch as he gazed on her, they both were shocked to be able to see each other. Ann's brain screamed 'shit! shit! shit! shit!' as she fought to control her breathing. Logan was gorgeous, even looking exhausted.

Ann swallowed, "Um Hi Logan!" Ann's voice came out a little more high pitched than she wanted it to, a deep blush painting her face. She realized in her camera feed she still had the towel on her hair and her breasts were just about swelling out the top of the form fitting tank top. Ann undid the towel, seeing his eyes watching her intently, as her blonde hair fell down her shoulders.

"Hey Ann, how are ya?" Logan drawled, Ann felt heat pooling in her pelvis at the deep accent. He was right when he'd mentioned in his letter that the first few moments of them talking would be awkward.

"I'm good. Just got out of the shower. Seems like you just did the same. What time is it over there? Shouldn't you be getting to bed?" Ann couldn't help stating the obvious, her brain to mouth connection was on the fritz.

Logan chuckled, a smirk crossing his lips, "Darlin' it's a bit past midnight here. I don't sleep much anyway given the recent events. I'd rather miss sleep to spend time with you."

Okay, now Ann was really blushing. He was willing to go without sleep to talk to her. That *was* something. She remembered telling him in her letter that she didn't care if he woke her to call her and that was true. She just didn't think it would be the same with him, especially being in Iraq.

"Oh. Well, I guess that makes sense. I was so scared for you when you said you had been attacked and Bonnie died in your arms. I'm so very sorry. Please let me know if you can when you go out next so I don't worry so bad ok?" Ann could feel the tears welling in her eyes once more, she blinked rapidly, hoping he wouldn't see them.

"Aw sweetheart, don't cry. I'm okay, just a little messed up in my emotions. It's something that's inevitable over here. I'll do my best to let you know somehow when I go out next ok? There's only so much I can do from here that won't get me in trouble." Ann saw his chest tighten as he sighed; he'd caught her trying not to cry. At least he wasn't making fun of her being emotional.

"How about we plan on you coming out to California and meeting me when the flight comes in? If things go well for that weekend, then we can plan a horseback getaway in the fall. Right now though, it's more important to me that we work on what we're building than getting too far ahead of ourselves if you're okay with that?" Logan had a point, they needed to focus on here and now and less on what was to come.

Ann nodded, taking a drink from her glass of water. "I agree we need to work on what we're trying to build. From here on out, it's me and you. The past is the past right?" Ann's stomach flopped when she thought back to Dustin in bed with her just yesterday morning; the past had to be put away if they were going to make this work.

"Yeah, me and you. No one else. Past is past. We can talk about it, but it ain't making an impact on us." Logan's feed flickered for a second, but the audio was clear. Ann could hear him in her mind talking her to sleep, his voice was so comforting to her, making her feel instantly at ease.

Looking back behind him on the messy bed, Ann could see her blue pillowcase. He hadn't lied saying it was on his bed and he was sleeping with it. She smiled seeing his eyes follow hers, as his back turned.

Ann sucked in a breath seeing the smattering of scars marring his back. She couldn't imagine someone inflicting that kind of pain on someone like Logan. He was so kind, and genuine, why someone would hurt him like that she couldn't understand. A tattoo of a Navy anchor lined down one side of his back, a Celtic cross on his ribcage and a Seabee outlined in rope on his left breast; he seemed to have *a lot* of tattoos. The tattoos didn't bother her as much as the scars though, she had to remind herself not to bring them up unless he started talking about them.

Logan must have seen the look on her face, his eyes softened as his voice was barely a whisper. "Yeah I told you I keep you on my bed with me. Ain't nothing dirty though, it just makes me feel better knowin' a piece of you is here with me."

"I know you don't mean anything dirty by it, it wasn't my intention for it to be dirty. I just wanted you to know that I care about you and you're in my thoughts. I worry about you that's all." Ann couldn't help the emotion in her voice, Logan didn't deserve the scars he had.

"Sweetheart, don't love me any less because of my scars. You're lucky I'm even letting you see 'em. Usually I don't let anyone see them. It's my past and we ain't letting the past influence us remember?" The corner of one side of Logan's lips turned up in a smile, trying to get Ann to look beyond the surface.

"I don't love you any less Logan, I'm glad you trust me enough to let me see you like this. The past is the past, it isn't us." Ann breathed out, seeing him instantly relax.

"Darlin', as much as I want to stay here looking at your beautiful face and talking to you, I gotta get to bed. Morning comes way too early here. Thanks for callin' me, means a lot to finally see you and hear your voice. Can we try again tomorrow night? I ain't gotta go in on Saturday, only thing I got planned for it is a rugby game." Logan smirked, making Ann smile. She could see herself in the feed on her side, the smile was bright and genuine.

"Um, yeah since it's almost 2am over there. I'm sure you have a lot to do for work tomorrow. Same time tomorrow night?" Ann saw him smile as he yawned, probably for effect more so than being tired.

"Yeah, I'll call you if I see you on. If not I'll check around the time you get back from school. Have a good day at school, and sleep tight sweetheart. Goodnight." Logan's voice had gotten quieter, Ann smiled as she leaned forward to click the mouse.

"Goodnight Logan, have a good day at work tomorrow." Ann disconnected the call, feeling empty inside. The conversation seemed awkward to her, but mostly because she hadn't known what to say. It felt as if Logan was saying everything she wanted to say, as if he was reading her mind.

Ann hummed to herself as she ordered dinner in from the local Chinese restaurant, thinking that this thing her and Logan were building just might work.

Fallujah, Iraq

Logan sat at the screen for a few minutes longer after Ann disconnected the call. He checked and made sure Navy Fed was set up to pay the bills like usual, but his mind was on Ann. He could tell she was shy talking with him for the first time, and emotional. Especially when she saw his scars-- that was something he would have rather her not seen if he had his way. At least his mind was put at ease, he and Ann were on the same page when it came to what they wanted to do with this relationship they were trying to build.

She looked absolutely beautiful straight out of the shower, even with a towel, wet hair and no makeup. That was fine with him, he liked his women natural. He hated when women felt compelled to pretty much sleep in makeup. That made them so fake to him, it was the wholesome girls that wore very little to no makeup that he went after. Ann's tank top fit a little bit too tight, he wasn't going to lie and say her eyes were the second thing he looked at when she flashed up on his screen.

Closing out the browser and powering down his laptop, Logan laid out his uniform for the next day. He set Ann's box next to his Oakley's and wallet, to remind himself to take it to the post office on his lunch hour. Logan stripped off the now dry towel hitched around his hips, pulling on a pair of boxer briefs before crawling into bed.

He looked over at Ann's pillow, thinking about how she was probably sleeping with the rest of the sheet set tonight in New York. Her face floated into his vision as he pulled that pillow tight into his chest, burying his nose in her fading scent. He'd never had a woman affect him like Ann did, probably because most of the women he fucked around with made it clear that was all they wanted from him. If it was made clear that was what they wanted, then he had no qualms of agreeing to it. But Ann was different, she wanted a relationship before sex. He really didn't think the distance had a damn thing to do with it, she didn't seem like the kind of girl to fuck and run.

Logan felt his eyes closing as he thought of Ann's voice telling him she cared about him, the emotion wrapped in her words genuine. Ann was something to hold onto, no matter what it took to do it.

Chapter Seventeen

Logan clutched the rugby ball to his chest, glancing across the makeshift dirt field that they played matches on. Logan had been playing rugby for nearly a decade, he'd picked it up when he found himself deployed with Marines in Spain. He relished the adrenaline of the game, it was a high similar to the one he got when he bagged an elk hunting. He spied Johnson off to his left and Smith to his right as he barreled up the middle heading for the goal.

Logan felt his feet come out from underneath him, his ass was airborne as the ball slipped out of his grip. Logan hit the ground hard, his breath seized in his chest, making him sputter and cough. When the black spots in his vision subsided, Logan was looking up into the shit eating grin of Paddy Flannery.

"And that boys is how ye stop a train! Come on brother, let's get ye up. Here ye go, easy now." Paddy grabbed

Logan by the forearm, hauling him up to a shaky standing position.

"That's game, Chief. Let's go get some chow." Johnson looked at Logan and Paddy both as Logan nodded. His face was tight with pain, Paddy had taken him down hard.

The crew of Seabees barged into the galley, laughing and talking as the rugby ball popped up in the air around them. Logan liked it when his guys were relaxed, they performed better and stayed focused on the job. Even Logan performed better after a game or talking to Ann. Something about that woman brought a calm to his soul, which Logan craved. He thought about trying to get ahold of Ann after he finished chow with the guys.

Looking at his watch, he realized Ann was probably just now eating lunch while he was eating dinner. The time difference was always a wrench in their relationship. Getting back to the states would make this relationship between them so much easier, the time difference wouldn't be so great and the communication wouldn't be so sporadic.

Logan shoved a forkful of what was supposed to be spaghetti into his mouth, chewing as he thought about Ann and the enemy of time. He was glad to know that the age between them made no difference to her, age wasn't the issue with them. The issue was time and distance, both of which neither had much control over at the present moment.

"Ye seem deep in thought Logan. Are ye okay? Didn'a take ye down too hard did I hmm?" Paddy's clear blue eyes settled on Logan's dog face, concerned for the man he considered brother. Logan had been angry around the time Mels left two weeks ago, but that anger had dissipated into something of a relative calm. Paddy knew Logan had a girl back in the states waiting on him, Logan had mentioned her briefly when Paddy went to his quarters and saw the picture taped to his desk lamp. Ann was a pretty girl, Logan was lucky to have her.

"I'm okay, just thinking about Ann and maybe trying to get a hold of her tonight. I know we talked the other night on Skype and I finally got to see her. But we missed each other last night. She was probably working or school or something. Don't expect her to put her life on hold for me." Logan cleared the last of the food on his plate as a box was tossed up on the table beside him.

Logan looked over to see Simmons' ass walking away from him, he swore if she'd been a horse that tail'd been swishing. Ever since Mels departure Simmons had been barking up Logan's tree, and she wasn't taking no for answer. Regs totally frowned on a relationship of such a far distance in rank, not that Logan would take her up on it anyway. Simmons seemed like the type who would bed anyone to get knocked up to get to go home.

Paddy whistled sharply, "Eh, someone's got her knickers in a knot now don't she? Girl's just looking for trouble if ye ask me." The Irishman shook his head, his attention on the box in front of them. "Looks like Ann sent ye a box. Wonder if there's some cookies in it? I'd go for a homemade cookie right about now. I'm wasting away over here ye know!"

"You're not wasting away you dirty bastard, you're just hankering for real food verses this shit we eat!" Logan laughed, cutting the tape on the box to find a dozen little bags of chocolate chip cookies in the box. Logan tossed two to Paddy, kept two for himself and whistled for his guys' attention. Heads turned as bags of cookies became airborne.

"You mangy fucks need to share you hear?" Logan hollered as the last bag was caught, heads nodded with calls of 'Yes Chief!' coming around bites of cookie.

"Aye, now that's a cookie. Sweet girl to send ye cookies every so often. Does she have a sister that's single?" Paddy waggled his eyebrows at Logan, savoring the bite of chocolate in his mouth.

"She does, but she ain't single no more. Here." Logan handed the envelope over to Paddy, who wiped his fingers on his pants before opening it.

"Aye. They're a beautiful pair of sisters. Looks like a wedding, they both look happy. Ann looks stunning in that red dress. Ye did good in finding her brother." Paddy handed the photos back to Logan, genuinely happy for the Stranahan sisters and Logan's good fortune with Ann.

"Didn't find her, she found me. And you're right, she's beautiful in red. I'm trying to get her to meet me in Hueneme when we come back. It's the least she and I can do after all these months of talking. Can't say I'm not nervous about meeting her though." Logan gathered up his tray and trash, tucking the cookies and the envelope of photos into his pants pocket.

Paddy followed Logan out into the cool of the night, walking towards Chief Row. "I wager it's natural to be nervous, but ye gotta admit that with both of ye talking like ye do, it should make the meeting that much easier."

Logan nodded, Paddy had a point. Ann had already admitted her feelings for him, and he knew the same kind of feelings ran within him. He just wasn't one to easily put those feelings to words. Logan unlocked his quarters, bidding Paddy goodnight as they shared in a manly shoulder hug. Paddy was the brother Logan needed and wanted, he didn't even think of his own blood brother much anymore. It seemed as if the Irishman had filled that void in Logan's life. If there was one person that Logan knew had his back, be it the deployment or outside of the Navy, right now it was a toss-up between Ann and Paddy.

Logan opened his Navy email first, finding an email from Mels. Logan was surprised that she was even emailing him, especially from her Navy.mil account. He clicked the subject line and began to read, his knee starting to tremble under his desk.

Dixon,

Thought I'd let you know that I got all my stuff out of the house in Cascade. Paid up the mortgage for next month, and called the bills for the month coming and paid those up for you. Stopped by and checked on the horses, they look real good. The Jensen kid's taking good care of them, made sure he was paid out for the rest of the deployment. I left my house and spare keys to your truck with Jensen as well. Figured it's the least I can do.

I got orders to ACB-2 in Little Creek, VA. Maybe if you ever come out that way we can do lunch or something for old time's sake. I hope you're keeping busy and staying sane over there, ain't much time left to go. Wish you the best with Ann, she's where you heart belongs. No hard feelings, trust me when I say that. Thanks for everything you've done for me, you're the best man I ever have had the pleasure of knowing.

Heiderschiedt

Logan blew out a breath, Mels was really gone from his life now. If he knew her like he did, she probably cleaned the house before she left, to make sure that she was well and truly gone from his life. He was thankful she checked on the horses, it made him feel better to know that his stock was in good hands. While Logan didn't need Mels to pay the mortgage or the bills, he understood why she did it. She wanted to walk away clean, what happened in Iraq had been the breaking point for her and all her bottled up emotions. She wanted him to have a life with Ann without the distractions of her, and she wanted to move on with her life without him. It felt like a divorce, the end of a marriage, not that Logan knew what that felt like. But that was what he compared it to in his mind. He'd been witness to plenty of his guys going through those over the years.

Logan closed out his work email, not even thinking of what to reply to Mels, he had no idea what to say to her if he was honest with himself. Logan opened his personal email, seeing a message from

Ann. His heart beat a little faster, any note from her made his day brighter.

Logan,

Hey sorry we missed each other last night. I got busy at the hospital and by the time I got home and cleaned up it was really late. I have plans to go out with Leah Saturday, but I'm sure you'll be able to call me and get me. I don't care if you wake me up, I'd go without sleep just to hear your voice again and know you're okay. It really makes me feel good when I hear from you, and it makes my day so much better. Call me tomorrow night.

Love,

Ann

Logan set his alarm clock to wake him up about six in the morning, so he could catch Ann before she went to bed. He was glad that she wasn't putting her life on hold for him, he didn't expect her to. That was a good sign, it meant that if they were able to make something out of this and be in it for the long term, he wouldn't have to worry about her when he deployed next.

Logan logged onto Expedia.com and pulled up flights. He found a flight coming in on the Thursday before they pulled in, Navy flights usually came in on Fridays from deployments so families could meet their loved ones for the weekend. With it being so close to May, Logan had a fairly close idea to when they would be coming in. He bought a flight leaving out of JFK at nine in the morning, and getting into LAX around noon. He was going to make sure Ann was waiting on the flight line for him, having the itinerary sent to his email. While it would only be a weekend that they would be together, Logan wanted it to be memorable and easy for Ann, and planning it ahead would ensure that. She would already be nervous as hell coming out to Cali to meet him, why make it any more stressful? Logan chuckled at his choice of rental car and hotel, knowing Ann would be shocked at it.

One charge to his credit card and the hotel, the flight and Ann's rental car was taken care of. Money didn't really matter to him at this point, he would have an entire deployment of pay in his bank account. This charge was a drop in the bucket for him, and it was for Ann, he didn't care that he spent two grand on her. She was worth it to him, she brought him back around from the darkness he was living in. He knew he loved her, he wanted to take care of her, and this was a gift to her. Logan just hoped she liked it when it all came through.

Chapter Eighteen

Ann cracked one eye open, hearing someone knocking loudly at her door. "Just a minute!" she called out as she tossed on her robe, hoping the person would wait the minute or so it would take her to get from the bedroom to the front door. Ann turned on her computer as she passed her desk to the front door. The person knocked one more time, just as she opened the door.

Ann was surprised to see Tom the postmaster grinning at her in the noon day light. He held out a small beat up box out, his hand shaking gently.

"Good morning Miss Stranahan. I'm running the mail out here today. Thought you'd like some mail from your Seabee. Makes me happy to see you two still going strong all this time. Reminds me of me and the Missus when I was deployed to Korea. Chief Dixon must be smitten with you sending him all those boxes of cookies. Fastest way to a man's heart is through his stomach." Tom joked as Ann took the box from him, her heart leaping in her chest.

"Thank you so much Tom. I really appreciate you bringing it to me. Logan's pretty special to me too." Ann couldn't hide the smile on her face; she wasn't expecting Logan to send her anything. This was a welcome surprise to brighten her day.

"I got to finish up my route. You have yourself a wonderful day Miss Stranahan." With that Tom tipped his hat and turned to walk away.

"You too Tom, have a great day. Thank you!" Ann called after the elderly postmaster, shutting the door behind her.

Ann skipped over to the kitchen counter, grabbing a knife out of the butcher block to cut the tape sealing the small box. As she pulled the top open, a distinct smell hit her senses. It smelled like the woods, dirt and a touch of grease.

The scent caused a tingle to spread down Ann's spine, centering in between her thighs. This was what Logan smelled like, the scent of her man making her tremble in anticipation of finally meeting him when he returned stateside.

Ann opened the box fully to find a note from Logan written in his blocky scrawl on top of a folded soft brown t-shirt. Ann pressed the shirt to her face, inhaling deep of his masculine scent. The heat pooled in her pelvis as she breathed Logan into herself.

She felt something metal poking through the shirt, Ann carefully unfolded the shirt as the metal object fell to the floor between her feet. Stooping to pick it up, her breath caught in her throat when she realized it was Logan's dog tags with a cross strung on the ball chain. She turned them over in her hand, reading the stamped words as her thumb lovingly caressed the metal. She had seen dog tags before, and knew what they symbolized. He was giving her a part of himself in the well-worn metal tags in her hand.

DIXON

LOGAN

466-23-9810USN

APOS

NO PREFERENCE

Now Ann knew they shared the same blood type, not that it mattered. What surprised her was that he had no religious preference. She couldn't understand why someone wouldn't have a religious preference, probably because she had been going to church since a young age, and it had always been a part of her life. It didn't matter to her that he wasn't religious; she did enough of that to cover the both of them. Ann looped the chain over her neck, careful to not catch her hair on it as the cool metal settled between her breasts.

Ann picked up the note, her eyes darting over Logan's words as her heart beat quickly.

Ann,

I know it ain't much on my end to send you this, but I wanted you to have something of me to bring you comfort when the nights get too lonely. Keep me close to your heart sweetheart.

Logan

Was this his way of saying they were committed? Sending her a piece of jewelry to wear was a sign to Ann he was serious about them. She laid the note next to her desk to remind her to email Logan and thank him for thinking of her.

Ann turned on the shower, stripping down as the water began to steam up the small bathroom. The shower woke Ann up even more, the hot water stinging at her skin. She could hear her phone ringing on the nightstand, hoping it wasn't Logan calling. Ann did some quick math in her head, realizing it was almost 8pm in Iraq; Logan was probably still hanging out with his guys at the rugby game.

Towel drying her hair, Ann walked around her bedroom naked. The cool early May breeze blowing through her bedroom window tickled her skin, causing goose bumps to prickle. The voicemail message reminder sounded, causing Ann to sit down and play the message.

"Hey girlie, haven't seen you in a couple of weeks. Thought we could go out today and do a girls day out. Text me and let me know! Love you!" Leah's voice filled the small bedroom; Ann smiled as she texted her best friend back. A girl's day sounded like the best idea Ann had heard in a while, her original plan for the day had been homework and cleaning the house she barely lived in as it were.

Ann's laughter turned to a gasp of surprise when Leah told her the story behind the new sapphire and diamond ring on *that* finger while they ate an early dinner. It seemed that the Navy recruiter that was canvassing campus for potential officer recruits had found the woman he wanted to spend the rest of his life with in Leah. Ann was genuinely happy for Leah, but also shocked that the one person she never thought would settle down was now engaged to a Lieutenant in the Navy. Ann sighed, thinking that maybe Leah was just doing it because of Logan, but then she remembered that Leah had been sniffing around the guy since October of the year before. It was entirely possible that Leah had fallen in love with the handsome officer within the last eight months.

Resentment bit at Ann's heels, Leah was in a totally committed relationship with a man she could talk to every night, could touch and make love to. Ann was resigned to missed phone calls, Skype, emails and letters. Her fingertips absently brushed the dog tags resting against her heart, thoughts of Logan pulling at her heart. Leah brought her out of her thoughts, thanking the waitress for the check that she promptly paid.

"Come on Ann, we're going shopping. I know just the thing to perk you up. Enough about me and Mike." Leah joked, grabbing Ann by the hand and leading her out of the Cheesecake Factory.

Ann looked at the huge red letters that made up the sign posted on the front of the building. She couldn't figure out for the life of her what the store carried, as Leah herded her to the front door.

"Come on Ann! I'll buy you something fun while we're in here!" Leah's voice was playful, making Ann wonder what the hell was in the store. Leah pulled Ann into the store, her face immediately flaming red of embarrassment.

"Leah! You have got to be kidding me!" Ann's voice held all the shock at the things lining the walls as Leah continued pulling her through the aisles. Ann was mortified at the items in her line of vision, having no clue what most of them were used for.

"Oh no Ann! You need some help in the getting laid department while your man's gone. There's nothing wrong with a little bit of self-love. It's safe sex, you can't get an STI or pregnant. Leave that to Logan when he gets home!" Leah burst out laughing at her own joke-- certain that near virginal Ann Stranahan was going to be pregnant before the year was out once Logan returned home.

"I'm not getting pregnant Leah, and I'm fairly certain Logan doesn't have an STI. I know what protection is for thank you very much." Ann stated plainly, watching as Leah pulled a gaudy colored box off the shelf, admiring the contents.

"This one is so you! It's cute and pink and just the right size. Trust me I have one just like it at home but in blue. It gets me off when Mike isn't around. I'm definitely buying you this one so you can soak your sheets!" Leah grabbed a bottle of clear fluid off the adjoining shelf before heading up to the check out. Ann was completely embarrassed, but even more so when the guy behind the counter asked Leah for her preferred customer card and then hit on Ann. Leah had a preferred customer card? How much did she shop there? The clerk even put batteries into the toy for Ann, who could feel the blush still on her skin. This was a whole new experience for her, and she wasn't about to tell anyone else about it, much less Logan.

Ann took her bag into her bedroom, opening the box and reading through the instructions on cleaning the phallic item with the bunny attachment. She set the bottle of what she now knew as a warming lubricant on the nightstand.

"Oh what the hell? Why not? It's not like I couldn't do without a good orgasm now and then. I'm sure Logan's been taking care of himself over there more than I have been taking care of myself here!" Ann admonished herself as she set about going into the bathroom and cleaning her new friend.

Ann had fallen asleep reading in bed, the sound of her phone ringing waking her. Looking over, she saw it was that 808 number, clicking answer as quick as she could. Static filled the line as Ann clicked on the speakerphone, "Hello?" her voice sounded sleepy even to her own ears.

"Hey Sweetheart, how are ya?" Logan's deep timbre came across the line clearly. Ann shivered, feeling the ache down deep hearing his voice. She had been dreaming about him, and those dreams were not pure of any means.

"I'm doing well, how are you Logan?" Ann's voice squeaked out, trying to hide the hum coursing over her skin.

"Can't complain. Did you have a good time out with Leah?" Logan smirked to himself as he looked across the base, seeing dust devils kicking up. He wished he was home in Colorado; elk season was coming on with it being the first of May. He thought about being in bed curled around Ann's warm body, breathing in her subtle floral scent. He tried to push that thought down, sporting a hard on in a public area wasn't the brightest idea at the moment. He watched as Marines and other Seabees passed by him, returning salutes to the non-rates who should have known they didn't have to salute him since he was occupied. Logan turned his face to the inside of the phone booth, leaning against the wall.

"Yeah, she took me out to dinner and I heard about her new fiancé'. He's a Navy officer recruiting here at our school. I'm happy for her. She took me shopping too." Ann swallowed, trying to ignore the thoughts flitting to the toy in her nightstand and the desire building in her pelvis at the sound of Logan in her ear.

"Uh huh, well at least she found an officer. Those butter bars make more than I do and work a helluva lot less. You got yourself a working man darlin', I work for the little bit I make. What'd you end up buying?" Curiosity got the best of him; two women going out shopping together couldn't ever prove to be a good thing. Trouble if you asked him what he thought about it.

Ann breathed out, reaching into the drawer of the nightstand, taking the heavy pink toy into her small hand. Hearing him ask about what she bought spiked excitement through her. And Logan calling her darlin' made her nipples ache against the bed sheet. She had to do something about this, or she was going to lose her mind trying to fight off the urge. Ann smeared some of the lubricant onto the toy, slowly inserting it. She couldn't bite back the throaty gasp that escaped her lips.

"Ann, you alright honey?" Concern laced Logan's voice, turning Ann on even more. The vibrations were purring through her now aching clit and soaking wet pussy making her shiver and moan. To hell with keeping quiet, there was no way with how her heart was beating inside her ribs and the rush of her body crashing towards her orgasm.

Yeah I'm okay Logan, just talk to me okay?" Ann gushed; hoping the desire for him in her voice made it through the phone lines. Knowing he had a clue as to what she was up to would be so dirty, yet exciting. Ann wasn't always miss prim and proper, as much as people thought she was.

"I'm so glad that me and the boys got to play rugby. You know it's one of those things that's not so fun to *play by yourself right babe*?" Logan emphasized the last part of his thought, a low growl coming out behind it. He had an idea of what Ann was doing in bed; the sounds she was making were loud and clear in his ear half a world away.

Ann's eyes popped open, hearing that lusty growl through the phone pushed her over the edge. He *knew* what she was doing and he *acknowledged* it.

Ann gasped out his name as the orgasm surged through her, she could feel the trembling of her thighs, the wetness coating the insides. She couldn't believe what she just did with Logan listening half a world away, but she felt better.

Logan grinned, crooking the phone in his shoulder to discreetly adjust himself. "You feel better sweetheart? I guess that explains what you bought today huh?"

Ann rolled over gingerly, feeling the aftershocks in her belly as the sheets brushed against her bare skin. She took the phone off the nightstand and clicked the speakerphone off. She wanted to hear his voice close to her heart.

"Yes. I feel better, thank you for helping. And yeah, Leah bought it for me. By the way, thanks for the shirt and your dog tags, you really didn't have to send them to me." Ann was nearly breathless, her body was slow in coming down from her orgasm.

Logan chuckled to himself, he was glad she had some way of finding release that didn't involve another man. It made him feel even better that he was able to help Ann cum; god knew it was a natural need for woman and man.

"Ann, honey, I wanted you to have mc with you when you get lonely. A lot like your pillowcase does for me. And you're welcome by the way."

"I have your tags on now, I hope that doesn't bother you. It makes me feel closer to you." Ann's fingers idly played with the black rubber gaskets, rubbing the thin metal disks together.

If Logan was honest with himself, he would admit that he was a bit jealous of his dog tags at the moment, as he was sure they were lying between her perfect breasts. "Nah, I want you to feel me there with you. It won't be much longer before I'm home. But I got a trip or two to take in between then and now, so we're gonna have to email for a little bit before I go and then things are gonna get a good bit quiet for a while ok?"

Ann felt her heart drop as she realized he was talking about going out on a project, and that things would be hard as he wouldn't have contact with her. How long he was going to be gone was unknown, as he wouldn't be able to tell her that.

"You be careful Logan and come home to me in one piece you hear? I love you." A tear slipped down Ann's check when she made what she knew to be true in her heart known to him.

"I will sweetheart promise ya that, and I know."

Chapter Nineteen

Logan watched as the trucks loaded up to head out to the project, *without him*. He'd lucked out, Johnson volunteered in his place since the crew was going back out to Baharia again. Johnson knew what had happened out in Baharia last time, he didn't want Logan to come apart and go nuclear on someone with his emotions about that site running high. Logan shook hands with Johnson, sending him out to load up in the last truck. While Logan knew staying behind was best for him, he still hated not going with his guys.

Logan puttered around the shop, checking through the work logs, signing off on things he knew were completed and working up the logs on what needed to be completed. Feeling his ass getting numb, Logan got out of the desk chair stretching. He felt his back and chest pop, making him groan. He knew he wasn't getting any younger, forty was just around the corner. Smirking at his own thoughts, Logan headed out into the shop. Looking through the faces, he realized the day shift had turned over into the night shift. Logan sought out his other half, the always genial Paddy Flannery.

Logan found him under a Humvee, squatting down to Paddy's level. "You need some help on this one?" Logan called under the truck, seeing the Irishman's head jerk up and bang into the under plating with a loud thunk!

"Fuck me, what in the hell are ye still doing here Dixon? Shouldn't ye be out on the convoy that just left out?" Paddy rolled out from under the truck, rubbing where his head had hit the plating.

Logan shook his head, not wanting to explain why he wasn't going out with the rest of his guys. "Nah, Johnson went out for me. He needs to prove he's up to snuff for First Class since Mels is gone. You got anything for me to work on for a bit? I need something to do with my hands."

"Aye, Johnson needs to be the big man on campus and get that next chevron. Did ye ever hear where H-12 landed at? If ye check the logs, I might have something for ye. But wouldn't it be better ye went and called that lovely girlfriend of yers instead?" Paddy could see the tension in Logan's posture, but being in the shop wasn't the place to burn that tension off at. Logan needed to spend some time with Ann, in any means available to them. Paddy knew a deployment wife wasn't an option, Logan wasn't that kind of guy.

"Got an email from her the other week, she's up in Little Creek with ACB-2. It's a good place for her, somewhere new. I'm sure Ann's still at school or something." Logan glanced at his watch, seeing it was almost midnight his time, making it around five in the evening in New York. Ann could be home, there wasn't any harm in taking the chance to see.

"Go on brother, give that beautiful lass a call before I do. Get ye ass on out of here." Paddy kicked at Logan's feet, knocking him off balance. Logan caught himself by reflex, kicking up to his feet.

Paddy laughed out loud, "Gettin' quicker old man."

Logan socked Paddy in the shoulder, "Ain't as old as you are." Smirking as he walked out of the shop, heading towards his quarters.

Logan logged into Skype, seeing Ann logged on. He parked his ass in the desk chair, not even taking the time to change out of his uniform. Within seconds of the call connecting, he saw Ann's beautiful face flash across the screen. Her hair was down around her shoulders, the green tank top making her blue eyes shimmer. He saw the chain of his dog tags looped around her delicate neck, the tags were inside her tank top. Ann beamed at seeing him, he was a sight for sore eyes, even with dirt and grease on his handsome face.

Logan couldn't help but smile back at her, she looked so very happy. "What are you so happy about honey?" He had a good idea why, she thought he was going out on a project and he wasn't. That alone would make anyone happy, especially Ann.

"I thought you were going out Logan? What happened are you ok?" Ann could hear the concern in her own voice, seeing him crook an eyebrow. She hated the thought of him being hurt to not be able to go out with his guys. Ann knew he held the responsibility for his guys high, and would hate not being with them.

"I'm okay Ann, just that Johnson took my place since they were going back out to Baharia. He needs to step up and get his shit in order for First Class. I got faith in him to do alright though. So with me coming back in less than eight weeks, what's on your mind?" Logan saw Ann's eyes light up; it was the first time he had mentioned anything that resembled a date of him getting back to the states.

Ann squeaked with joy, "Eight weeks? Really? I need to look at flights and stuff to meet you in Colorado then. I have internship up to the first week in July at the VA starting Monday. So I don't know when I will see you next." She couldn't be happier knowing the countdown was less than eight weeks until she could see Logan and finally be able to touch him. That would make her year, touching the man she loved for the first time and breathing in that scent she indulged in when she felt lonely at night.

"Internship at the VA? Why the VA? Guess that means you're getting close to graduation then?" Logan thought back to one of her first letters, saying she had about a year and half at that point before she graduated. Most of that year had passed by since they started talking back in November. It was now the third week of May, he had just two months of the deployment left. There was one project left on the board, and it would be time to start the drawdown to go home.

"Yeah, I want to work with veterans coming back from the war, specifically Neurology cases. Brain injuries are destroying their lives and that of their loved ones. It's the least I can do for what they give up for us. I graduate next May. You gonna be there at my graduation?" Ann figured if everything went well with them that Logan would be there to see her become a doctor.

Logan smiled at his girl, "Ann, you know I promised you I'd be there to see you graduate. I ain't gonna break a promise to you." He was so proud of her being so close to graduation, not many people he knew finished high school, much less a doctorate degree.

Ann got a sly grin on her face at that comment. "What else is on your mind Logan?" Her thoughts began circling back to the phone conversation they had about two weeks ago, as she felt her skin warm and wetness seep into her panties. The thought of him knowing she was masturbating, as well as having no problem with it turned her on.

His eyes turned almost a midnight blue as his accent got thicker, "That phone call the other week between us. Girl, you put me in a helluva position being at a public phone. Hearing you moan and all breathless, can't say it didn't get me hard as steel. Someday I want to hear that for myself and feel my fingers on your skin."

Ann bit back a small gasp, he was thinking about the same thing she was. Swallowing hard, her eyes met his through the screen. "Well, since you're in your room and I'm at home how about we play a little game?" Ann hoped he would be onboard, she needed a release, and it wasn't fair for either of them to think these thoughts without release.

"Mhm, what kinda game you got in mind Ann?" Logan could see where her mind was going with the flush of her skin. The thoughts of her naked in bed with that toy flooded his mind, he could feel himself stir in his uniform pants. He purposely made his voice low, knowing it made her get hot.

Ann cleared her throat, chuckling nervously. "How about a game of 'I've Never' with a twist?" Ann saw him cock an eyebrow as a slow grin crept across his features.

"You got my attention darlin'. What's the twist?" Logan had a pretty good idea what it was, but he wanted to hear it from his good little girl's mouth. He had a sneaking suspicion that under the prim and proper exterior there was a dirty girl in hiding.

"If you lose the round, you lose a piece of clothing, simple as that. Who's starting?" Ann took a long drink of the glass of water on her desk, his eyes meeting hers.

Logan nodded at her, "Ladies first." This was going to be payback for what she put him through the other week. He was sure she was burning to see what he had to offer, and he would make her work for it.

"Okay, that's fair. I've never been to another continent." Ann smiled, knowing he was losing that one right off. She wasn't going to lose this game, it was her full intention to see Logan in all his naked glory if she had her way. Ann just had to think of the right things and play off of Logan, if he played fair.

Logan stood up, unbuttoning the blouse that covered his uniform tee. Ann had a view of only the chest as his fingers popped the buttons one by one. A slight chuckle vibrated in his chest, seeing her eyes watching him intently as he undid the last button and smoothed his t-shirt against his abs for her pleasure. Logan dropped the blouse down on the floor next to his chair, taking back his seat at the screen. He had to think up something that would be an easy win for him, nothing could be more easy than the obvious.

"I've never been to college." A squeak of being caught came across the line as Ann's nose wrinkled. Logan thought it was cute. "What's it gonna be darlin'?"

Ann sighed; knowing she started the game, so she needed to play along. She stood up; if she was going to do it, she was going to go big. The steel grey yoga pants slithered down her hips, all Logan could see was dark green lace panties against her nearly flat stomach. He felt himself get hard, running a hand down over his face. He knew Ann could see his eyes growing wide, hearing her giggle was music to his ears.

"I take it you like what you see?" Ann grinned into the camera as she bent down to finish getting the pants off, giving him an eyeful down her tank top. He could see his dog tags between her breasts. It was all he could do to swallow and nod, shifting a bit in his chair.

Ann sat back down in her chair, dropping the yoga pants off to the side of her own chair. "I've never been so drunk that I couldn't remember what I did that night."

"Fuck" Logan groaned, yanking his t-shirt over his head. Ann felt the heat pooling in her pelvis, Logan without a shirt was serious eye candy. Her eyes ran over his skin, nodding her approval. "Guess we're one for one huh?"

"Yep. So I have on panties, dog tags and a tank top. You're at pants, boots, underwear right?" Ann couldn't keep the smile off her face, she really had to play the game to get him naked, since he had on more than she did.

"Yeah, but in the idea of fairness, boots and socks count as one." Logan was going to be a gentleman and give her that one. It made the odds equal in his mind, as equal as they could be at least. But he wasn't a man who liked to lose either.

"I've never masturbated on the phone with someone." Logan pulled out the big guns shamelessly. Ann turned bright red, she couldn't deny the truth of what she had done with him. Logan grinned at catching her good.

"Damn it. You can't be serious! You're a sailor, you guys do all kinds of crazy stuff!" Ann watched his eyes as he t'sked, he was serious.

"I'm serious. I've never masturbated on the phone with someone. And I'm a Seabee sweetheart, there's a difference between me and them fleeters." Logan watched as her arms pulled inside the tank top straps, the hem of the shirt coming up her ribs. His eyes trained on that screen, seeing perfect pink nipples tipping her perfect pert breasts. He watched as his tags flopped onto her chest, making that metallic clink sound. If he thought her beautiful before, now he thought she was absolutely gorgeous. His cock agreed with his brain, coming at full attention in his pants.

"Yours Logan. You like?" Ann could feel her hormones rushing through her body, here she was sitting practically naked in her living room with Logan's eyes eating her alive half a world away. She'd be lying if she said she wasn't horny as hell at the moment.

"Sexy as sin baby doll." Logan drawled, not even trying to hide the desire in his voice. He knew he wanted her, and he wanted her to know without a shadow of a doubt that he found her desirable.

Ann blushed at his words, the tone of his voice shooting straight to the soaking wet flesh between her thighs. She shuddered hard as she thought of the next one to catch him at. It had to be dirty, had to be sinful. It had to be something personal, she wanted a reaction from him that would light her on even more. It had to be gasoline to her fire, she wanted this man with every fiber of her being.

"I've never had a threesome." Ann breathed out, almost a whisper. Logan's eyes locked with hers for a moment, as he swallowed hard. Ann watched as he slowly rose up, his fingers unlatching his rigger's belt and starting down the buttons of his pants. Ann could see the vee of his abs and the slim of his hips as his fingers hooked into the waistband of his pants. She could clearly see the heavy bulge of his erection pushing the flaps of the fly apart. Just as the pants started to shimmy down his hips, Ann drew a sharp breath.

"Stop! As much as I want to see you naked Logan, I want to wait till I see you. I want to touch you for myself." The tone of her voice hit Logan in the chest, she was embarrassed. He couldn't understand why, as he sat back down in the desk chair. Ann's eyes blinked, her breath was coming out in short gasps.

"You ok honey? We ain't gotta go no farther if you ain't comfortable. Good things come to those who wait." Logan was trying to think of a topic to bring the conversation back around to, something more innocent than sex.

Ann sat there in just her panties, she didn't have a problem with him seeing her topless. They were just boobs for god's sakes. But the thought of her seeing his cock via webcam was just a bit too far for her. Ann fought to slow her breathing, but the hum of her blood running through her veins was getting the best of her.

Logan was the first to speak, "Ann, honey. I know you ain't gonna like hearing this, but I got one last project to go on and I'm gonna be gone the entire month of June. I'll be back in time to do the drawdown and pack up before we head home. This one's at a remote base out by the Syrian border. Won't be able to get in touch with you till I get back here." He saw her eyes mist over, it wasn't the direction he wanted to take the conversation, but he needed to diffuse the situation a bit.

Ann nodded, feeling her emotions turning from lust to sadness. She knew the fighting in Anbar province was getting bad, and with him being way out by the Syrian border made her that much more afraid for him. Ann took a drink out of her glass, Logan saw her hand shake just a little bit as the glass met her lips.

"Baby, I promise you, I'll be okay. Just email me when you need to talk to me. I'll get them when I get back and respond to you. Don't worry about me ok?" Logan wanted to reach out and touch her, to assure her that he would be fine. But that was the problem with being half a world away, he couldn't touch her.

Ann nodded, "I'll email you while you're gone then. I need to go get some dinner arranged, and you need to get some sleep. I love you Logan. Be safe."

"I know. I will Baby girl. Get you some dinner. Sleep well." Logan watched Ann's chest heave as she leaned over to click the mouse, disconnecting the call.

Logan ran a hand over his grimy face, seeing grease come back on his hand. It was time for his shower before bed. That was his thing, he couldn't go to sleep without a shower, at least not here in hell. Stripping out of what was left of his uniform, Logan noticed he was still half hard. Seeing Ann's big blue doe eyes, her hair tickling her nipples and his dog tags against her skin in those last moments before she disconnected the call stirred thoughts in him.

Logan turned the knobs over to hot, his fingertips threading through the water to get it to just the right temperature. Finding a suitable temperature, Logan leaned against the shower wall, letting the water cascade over his back and shoulders. He closed his eyes; his thoughts drift back to the phone call with Ann as he helped her orgasm. The sounds in his memory mixed with the visual of her nearly naked tonight on Skype came together. Logan could see her writhing in her bed, sheets twisted around her body as she was making herself cum. All blonde hair, soft skin, pursed lips and breathless.

He could almost feel her skin under his hands, his lips wrapped around her nipple as his fingers glided down her body to dip between her thighs. Logan grasped his turgid length in his hand, letting the scene play in his mind as he brought himself closer to a crashing orgasm. Logan growled as he heard Ann call his name out through her orgasm, the memory pushing him over the edge, his body shaking against the shower wall.

He needed to get home to Ann, he needed to show her how much he needed her, how much he loved her.

Chapter Twenty

Ann kicked off her shoes and headed directly for the shower after getting home from the VA. A line of dirty clothes followed behind her as she walked towards the bathroom, and Ann didn't give two shits about cleaning it up. She never thought how much a hot shower could make her feel better, but the heat and spray helped with the ache in her back and neck from pouring over patient files with the Neurology team today.

Ann walked through her apartment, the breeze blowing through tickled her skin, making her sigh in contentment. Summer in New York wasn't too terrible, especially for the beginning of June. Ann pulled Logan's soft brown tee shirt over her head, savoring the feel and his barely perceptible scent. It made her feel closer to him, even with them being half a world apart still.

Sipping the Jameson and coke at her desk, Ann clicked the mouse to bring the computer to life. Within seconds, her email pinged making Ann aware she had new email. Sifting through the usual emails of social gatherings going on at school she didn't have time for, sales at Yankee Candle Company and the newest line at Victoria's Secret, Ann saw two emails from Logan.

Her heart sang in her chest to see email from him, any contact from him made her day brighter. The first email was short and to the point, it didn't take Ann long to read it.

Ann,

Time's getting short. Gotta go on vacation for a month, can't wait to see you when I get back. You've been on my mind more than you'll ever know.

Logan

The second email was an attached document, which Ann's computer already scanned for viruses before it let her download it. It was a PDF file, Ann took a drink as it was uploading, and nearly spit what was in her mouth out on to the keyboard and screen when she realized what she was looking at. The whisky burned going down, she'd just about choked on it reading the document.

The page stated that she had a nonstop flight from JFK leaving on Thursday, July 10th at 11:30am to arrive in Los Angeles at 220pm. The Virgin America flight returned on Sunday, July 13th from Los Angeles at 11:30pm to arrive back at JFK at 7:55am that Monday July 14th. Ann knew she would have to skip clinical on Monday, but it was worth it to spend even the weekend with Logan. A rental car was set up for her to pick up at LAX, and a hotel room was in place in Oxnard, CA. A place called the Embassy Suites Mandalay Bay, which Ann quickly Googled. Her eyes popped at the pictures, the hotel was right on the beach and looked like something out of a movie rather than a hotel.

It was when Ann reached the bottom of the page that she saw how much Logan had plunked down for her to spend the weekend with him. She didn't think she was worth that much, or that she deserved it. But Logan thought that much of her, and if he thought that of her, then she would make every effort to be there for him. They were a couple now, and spending time together, no matter how small was what couples did.

Fallujah, Iraq

Logan shucked into his bulletproof vest, grabbing his M4 rifle and the rest of his gear. He walked with a purpose out to the convoy of trucks waiting for him to give the load out call to. The project they were heading to was on the Syrian border, a remote outpost that was being built up for Marines to take over. Logan's part in the work would include building a gate and lookout towers with a crane crew. Project time slated was a month, they had 30 days to get the gate built, the lookout towers built and the base secured before the crew was to return to Fallujah to initiate the beep for the incoming battalion.

"Alright! Let's saddle up and get on the trail!" Logan called as he walked up to the lead vehicle, slinging up into the back to sit with the rest of the leadership. He wasn't one to rub elbows and kiss asses, but as a Chief this was his designated spot in the convoy. Logan grumbled looking at the other Chief in the rig with him, and the wet behind the ears Ensign. That was all he needed, a kid on his first deployment and the tight ass of the battalion with him. This was going to be a real good time.

Logan pulled his IPod out of the pocket of his pants, plugging in the ear buds to drown out the chatter of the other Chief and the Ensign, as well as the drone of the truck. He could feel the photo of Ann pressed against his chest through the t-shirt, the body armor compressing his blouse to his chest. His thoughts wandered to what time it was in New York, glancing at his watch. It was around 7am EST, meaning Ann was probably already at the hospital seeing patients. Logan grinned to himself, he was so proud of Ann for going to medical school.

Time passed so slowly, especially when you were looking forward to something. He couldn't wait to see Ann in California in just six short weeks. Before they had rolled out of Fallujah, Logan had sent Ann the travel info via email. He hoped it would be enough to keep her holding on through this month of no contact. Logan focused on the music filling his ears. The sounds of Chris Young's "It Takes a Man" lulled Logan into a heavy sleep as the convoy headed towards Rawah.

Elmsford, New York

Ann sucked a heavy breath as the tears ran down her face in the middle of the night. Her fingertips brushed angrily at the tears that woke her from the nightmare that still plagued her. Ann felt her body tremble, it would be a bit before she would be able to go back to sleep. Getting out of bed, she lumbered into the kitchen, sniffling as she opened the door to the refrigerator. Looking inside, Ann found her leftover sushi and orange chicken. She smiled thinking of her sister, emotional eating was the one thing they had in common. Ann threw the orange chicken in the microwave, mowing through the sushi as the chicken warmed up. Who needed chopsticks at 2am? Sushi could be finger food right?

Sitting down at her desk, Ann logged into her school email, hoping to see something from Logan. But knowing it was now the last week of June, and he was gone on the project that he would have no way of contacting her. Ann pulled a piece of paper out of the printer, her eyes glancing over the travel info that Logan had emailed her three weeks prior. Pulling a pen out of her desk drawer, she ate with one hand while words began to appear on the paper underneath her hand. By the time Ann finished the plate of leftovers, the front of the page was full and she was beginning to work on the back. By the time the page was half full, Ann signed off in her usual flourish. She tucked the letter into an envelope and addressed it to Logan, before heading back to bed.

One thing they always expected of each other was honesty, and Ann wasn't about to change that.

Rawah, Iraq

Logan was ground guiding the loader onto the trailer, getting it centered to be chained down for the trip back to into Fallujah. He heard the distinctive whistle of the RPG before he saw the explosion. It hit a truck about 60 feet away, tearing the stake truck apart. Logan was blown back into the trailer, his bell rung as he hit the steel side rail of the trailer. Logan fought to open his unfocused eyes to see people scrambling, the sound of gunfire muffled in his ears as the ringing charged to the front, making him want to retch.

Logan lurched to his feet, pulling the .45 pistol out of his thigh holster. He staggered towards some of his guys, who were crouched down behind another truck taking cover. Logan was about to bark out the orders when he was thrown back to the ground, white, hot searing pain ripped through his nerve endings, making him scream out in pain.

Blinking through the pain, Logan looked up into the concerned face of CM3 Davidson, seeing blood on the young man's face. "Hang on Chief, I got ya. CORPSMAN! Someone get the fucking Doc!" Davidson yelled over his shoulder, keeping his hand pressed to the wound in Logan's chest.

Logan struggled to push words out, finding he had difficulty breathing. Each breath was harder to take, the pain overloading his senses. Within seconds the face of HM1 Ingram swam into Logan's vision, as CMCN Reynolds tore Logan's body armor off.

"Call me in a medevac, I'll treat this here as best as I can." Doc Ingram cut through Logan's blouse and t-shirt, rolling him over to look for an exit wound.

"No exit Doc, just an entrance." Davidson was the second set of hands for Ingram, who pressed sterile dressings to the wound to try and stop the flow of blood.

"Keep pressure there, hang on Chief. I got you. One lung's down. Fuck, it's a sucker! I need that helo in now!" Ingram pulled out a chest wound kit from her crash bag, ripping it open with her teeth. "Davidson, get the space blanket out of my bag and get it on him. Don't need him crashing out on me!"

Ingram smoothed the adhesive side of the disk over Logan's chest, seeing the Chief's breathing almost immediately improve as the distinctive sound of rotors on a Sea King cut through the cacophony of the chaos. Davidson pulled the blanket up to Logan's chest, Corpsmen from the helo came running with a stretcher, loading Logan onto it before hauling him into the helo with Ingram.

Logan's hand shot out, fisting Ingram's shirt collar, making the Doc interrupt her work starting an IV and to look at him. "Picture. Blouse pocket." Logan croaked out through bloody lips. Ingram nodded, digging through the pocket, flipping Ann's blood stained picture over. Logan smiled, "Flannery, call her."

"I'll let him know myself as soon as we land in Fallujah and you're into surgery Chief. I promise." Ingram gripped Logan's hand tight, watching the morphine pull him under into the darkness of sleep. She took note of the writing on the back of the photo, the name, address, email address and phone number of a girl by the name of Ann Stranahan, who Ingram assumed was the petite blonde in the photo.

Fallujah was a good thirty minutes by helo, they had been lucky that the responding crew had been taking medical supplies to Fallujah and they were on the way. Now it was a gamble if Logan was able to make it back to Fallujah, Ingram hadn't lost a patient yet, and she wasn't about to start.

Landing in Fallujah, Ingram made sure Logan was on the way to the CASH before heading to the shop to seek out Flannery. Stepping into the shop, she started calling out his last name. Heads turned and fingers pointed, Ingram following the signs as she continued yelling.

"Aye! That's me!" Paddy yelled, looking up from a hydraulic system he was helping another CM fix to see a bloody female Corpsman holding a photo in her hand.

"Chief Dixon told me to give this to you. He wanted you to notify her." Ingram swallowed hard as she handed the blood-stained photo over to Flannery.

Paddy took the photo with shaking hands, seeing the face of Ann Stranahan looking back at him through the smudges. He flipped the photo over, seeing all of the contact info scribbled in Logan's blocky script.

Paddy swallowed thickly, "Is he ok?"

"He was stable when we got airborne. I did my best to keep him comfortable on the ride over. Wasn't an easy haul. He's over at the CASH now." Ingram turned to walk away, Paddy grabbed her elbow, turning her back around.

"Thanks Doc, he's me brother ya know." Paddy forced the tears in his eyes to not fall.

"I know Chief. Dixon's one of the best." Ingram's eyes met Paddy's before she turned to walk away.

Paddy called off, running for the phone bank. Ann needed to hear it from someone closer to Logan than the ombudsman. That person was Logan's brother, Paddy.

Chapter Twenty One

Ann clawed the top of her nightstand, reaching for the phone that was ringing rather loudly. Looking at the clock, Ann noticed it was 3:30am, who the hell would have the balls to call her at that hour of morning? Logan was gone on the project still, so It wouldn't be him. Ann grumbled tapping the answer button and speakerphone, licking her dry lips.

"Hello?" She croaked, hoping that it came across to the person on the other end that they were interrupting her sleep cycle. She had to be up in two hours to be at the hospital to see patients in the ER; it was part of her rotation for internship.

The all too familiar sound of static filled the line, as Ann clicked the screen to see it was that 808 number, her heart pounding in her chest to get to talk to Logan.

"Ann? Ann Stranahan?" The Irish accent coming across the line was not Logan, whomever it was sounded like they were upset.

Ann sat up in bed, clicking off the speakerphone and bringing the phone up to her ear. "Yes, this is Ann. Um, who's this?" Her heart and mind reeled with the thoughts of why someone other than Logan would be calling her from Iraq. Was he injured? Had he been killed? Was he playing some joke on her just to see what she would do? It was then that Ann remembered that Logan had put her down as the person to be notified if something happened. But wasn't the ombudsman's name Amy? The voice on the other end was most certainly male and calling from Iraq.

"I'm CMC Paddy Flannery. Me brother, CMC Logan Dixon, asked me to call ye. Are ye sitting down love?" Paddy took a long drag of the cigarette hanging precariously between his fingers. It had been years since he'd last smoked, but with the given situation, Paddy had no problem bumming a smoke off the non-rate in the booth next to him.

Ann's mouth went dry, nodding to the phone. She almost smacked herself in the head realizing Paddy couldn't see her nod. "Yeah Paddy, I'm sitting down. Is Logan ok?"

"Sorry for waking ye Ann, I forgot about the time difference. Logan was wounded today out at the project. I don't know how bad it is; the Corpsman just came and notified me in the shop. She had yer picture in her hand, which Logan had on him. Was how I got yer information to call ye." Paddy took another drag, the cigarette trembling in his fingers.

"Please tell me he's not on a one way ticket through Germany. Is he in surgery?" Words rushed out of Ann before she could even think, she wanted to get on a plane to Baghdad and find her way into Fallujah to be at Logan's side. She didn't know the stipulations for getting sent home through Germany. She knew a heart attack was serious enough, but without knowing how bad Logan was injured, she couldn't make an educated guess.

"Ingram said he was in surgery, so he won't be going through Germany. I haven't went and checked on him yet, I thought it was more important that I came and notified ye Ann." Paddy paused to take the last drag of the smoke, his eyes searching the Marines walking past him to bum one more. He grinned seeing a Lance Corporal walking up to the phone next to him. Paddy mimed a smoke, the LCpl gladly handing the coffin nail over along with his Zippo.

Paddy took a calming drag as he heard Ann quietly sobbing on the other end. God, if he could reach through the phone and pull his brother's woman into his arms to bring her comfort he would. Damn them being half a world apart during times like these.

"If he's awake when you go see him, please tell him I love him and that I can't wait to see him in Cali. I know it's only like three weeks away now and he's paid for everything for me to be there. I damn well plan on being there to greet him on the flight line!" Ann realized then that she had finally put into words the feelings she only shared with Logan to someone else. These feelings she had for Logan were real now, Ann couldn't hide them anymore.

Paddy grinned; knowing hearing those words out of his mouth would make Logan give him a weird look. "I will love; ye got me word on it. I'll call ye again when I find out how he is or if he's out of surgery. Take care of yerself and try and have a good day okay?"

"Thank you for calling Paddy. I'd rather of heard it from you than someone else. If you don't get ahold of me, please leave me a message ok?" Ann breathed out a sigh of relief knowing that Paddy would keep her up to date on Logan's status. She made a mental note to herself to seek Paddy out in Cali and thank him properly for taking care of Logan.

"I will love. Yer welcome. I gottta go." Paddy extended his goodbye to Ann as he hung up the phone.

Ann walked into the kitchen, Logan's dog tags cool against her bare skin. There was no point in trying to force herself to sleep. Her heart was thousands of miles away in a hospital on a military base. Ann popped a Kcup into her Keurig, listening to the familiar hiss of the machine brewing her morning cup of coffee. Seeing the letter she had wrote earlier in the night sitting on the bar next to her purse, Ann grabbed a pen and flipped the envelope over. *'I just miss you so much'* was quickly scribbled underneath the seal of the envelope.

Ann sipped the steaming mug of coffee, hoping that Logan would pull through surgery. She didn't know what she would do without him in her life. For being in her life such a short time, he had become a large part of her life, and took up a large space in her heart.

Fallujah, Iraq

Paddy walked into the CASH, striding right up to the Hospitalman's desk. The young girl looked up at Paddy, taking in the rumpled cammies, the anchors on the collar and the scowl that completed the look of a crabby Chief.

"Can I help you Chief Flannery?" HM3 Smith looked up from the paperwork she was finishing on the newest arrival to the recovery unit.

"Chief Dixon. Is he out of surgery?" Paddy couldn't help the gravel in his voice; his emotions were still on edge from talking to Ann, even with smoking through the entire conversation.

"Yes Chief, he's been back in the unit for about fifteen minutes now. I can take him to you." With that Smith led Paddy into the unit, past rows of beds containing other wounded service members. Paddy sucked a breath as Smith pulled a chair up next to the bed that Logan laid in.

Paddy took Logan's hand in his own as he sat down, Smith quickly turned on her heel, leaving the two men alone.

"Hey how ye doing there brother?" Paddy muttered, forcing a smile across his lips.

Logan's eyes fluttered open, taking in the worried guise of his Irish brother. He then tried moving his position in the bed to get more comfortable, but it wasn't without difficulty. Tubes and sensors were attached all over his bruised body, oxygen fed through his nose. "Help me sit up would ya?"

Paddy nodded, moving the bed into a sitting position as Logan grimaced. The staples in his chest didn't move with the rest of his body very easily, reminding him that he had been wounded. His thoughts took the direct route to Ann, hoping that Ingram had passed his message to Paddy to notify her of his injury.

"Ann, did you call her?" Logan looked at Paddy, seeing him nod slightly as he blinked away the wetness forming in his eyes.

"Aye did. She told me to tell ye that she loves ye and can't wait to see ye in Cali. Said nothing was gonna stop her from being on that flight line and greeting ye when we pull in. Ain't gonna lie and say she didn't cry when I told her what happened to ye." Paddy squeezed Logan's hand, getting the point across that he too was scared for his brother. Paddy needed Logan in his life to fill the void of his own blood brother Liam when they were younger. Logan reminded him so much of Liam, that sometimes Paddy caught himself almost calling Logan by Liam's name.

"Shit." Logan ran his hand over his face, his fingertips catching in the stubble growing on his chin and jawline. "I knew it would tear her up, but it would be worse coming from Amy. Don't know why that woman loves me the way she does, ain't like I'm nothing special." Logan couldn't keep the grin off his face. Knowing Ann loved him, and her willingness to admit it to someone else, made him feel good.

"It's 'cause she ain't met me yet. We all know I'm the better looking of the two of us." Paddy chuckled, seeing Logan wince as he laughed himself.

"Right, that's what it is. Fuck you for making me laugh by the way." Logan gritted his teeth as pain shot through his chest, his lungs burning.

"Eh, put yer big boy underoo's on and get better. That woman needs to see ye sooner than later." Paddy patted Logan's shoulder as he stood to leave.

Logan caught his brother's hand, as Paddy glanced back. "If you talk to Ann tell her I'm okay and I'm thinking about her will ya?" Logan was more concerned for Ann than he was himself. He could live with himself hurt, but he couldn't live with the thought of her being hurt.

"I will. Get some rest so ye can get out of here. I hate these kinda places." Paddy grinned as he left the recovery unit, heading for the Exchange to get a pack of smokes and a lighter before he called Ann again. She would be tickled to know that Logan was awake and thinking of her. If it was Paddy in Logan's shoes, he'd be happy as hell to have a woman worried about him back in the States. Hell, who was he kidding? Paddy would be happy as hell to have a woman, much less one worried about him.

Paddy was sitting down on a bench outside the Exchange as he tapped the

Camel Crush pack against his hand. Pulling the brushed stainless silver Zippo out of the bag, he slid the case off to fill the reservoir of the lighter. A few flicks of the wheel and the acrid bite of butane filled Paddy's lungs. Taking a cigarette out of the pack, he pursed it between his lips and lit the end. Taking a long drag, Paddy packed the small bottle of lighter fluid into the thigh pocket of his cammies, watching people walk past him going about their day.

He pulled Ann's bloodied photo out of the pocket of his blouse, looking over the information and Ann's gentle features. He could see why Logan was in love with her, she was a beautiful woman. Logan was a lucky son of a bitch to be with Ann, she seemed genuine and down to earth to Paddy.

"Hey Chief, can I bum a smoke?" Paddy looked up into the blue green eyes of HM1 Ingram, the small smile lighting up her face.

Paddy smirked, shaking out a smoke from the pack and lighting the Zippo for her. He watched as she took a deep breath, the nicotine and menthol making her eyes widen.

Ingram sat down next to Paddy, smoking in quiet next to him. He was shocked when she reached for the Monster in his hand as he was about to take a drink. Her fingers slid over his, as he relinquished his hold on the can. Watching as Ingram took a deep drink from the can; Paddy couldn't help but feel for the woman. She'd been back from a field trauma less than three hours and here she was sitting in the middle of a base sharing a smoke and a Monster with someone she hardly knew.

Ingram nodded at the photo, handing the Monster back to Paddy. "Did you give her a call for Dixon?" He could smell the menthol on her breath; they sat that close to each other.

"Aye did. She was glad to hear it from me, sad to know the news though. Went and seen him, seems he'll be okay. Ye did him good Ingram." Paddy took another drink of the Monster, handing the rest over to Ingram as he tucked the photo back in his blouse pocket.

"You're a good man Flannery. Any woman would be lucky to be on your arm." Ingram squinted up at the Irishman as he stood to walk away. "What'd you do before the Navy?"

Paddy smiled, tucking a fresh Camel behind Ingram's ear, his fingers sliding over her cheek. Ingram turned a bit into his touch, smiling tenderly.

"Chicago firefighter love. Have ye a good rest of the day." Paddy turned to walk away, hearing Ingram cough lightly.

If he was a betting man, he would bet that the little exchange between them was Ingram flirting with him. And if he was honest with himself, Paddy wouldn't mind getting to know Doc Ingram better.

Chapter Twenty Two

Logan had spent the better part of that first week in July turning things over to the new battalion coming in. He had made sure that all the equipment in the shop was ready for the new guys, as well as catching up the new Chief's on what was going on and what still needed repaired. He'd missed out on a good bit of what had been going on while he was in the CASH; the dull ache along his ribs a temporary reminder. Johnson had done a stellar job of keeping the shop running in his absence, especially with Paddy ready to help when he could. Logan couldn't have asked for a better crew that was for damn sure.

By the end of the second week, he had started packing up his room. While there wasn't much needing packed, he still needed to get it cleaned up for the next Chief coming in. He'd kept the pillowcase Ann had sent him, but left the rest of the bedding and furniture for the next Chief. He'd left the extra bathroom items Ann had sent him; he wouldn't have any need for them now that he was leaving. Once things were packed up, Logan slung his sea bag over his shoulders, and carried out his backpack with his laptop in it. Hearing that door lock behind him for the last time made him somewhat poignant, so many memories lived inside that room for him. A fleeting moment of thought passed on Mels, Logan missed his friend. He thought of giving her a call once he got stateside, just to let her know he made it back in one piece.

Logan dropped his sea bag off with the rest of the luggage, slinging his backpack over his shoulders. He turned in his rifle and sidearm, along with most of the other combat gear he still had in his possession. Turning in that gear meant time was coming very close to getting on that plane and flying into Kuwait. From Kuwait it would be London and into California. Almost two days on a plane would bring him into the states, and into Ann's arms.

A hand clapped over Logan's shoulder, turning his eyes onto his Irish counterpart. "Ye ready to do this dear brother? Blow this fucking shithole and getting back to whisky, women and beer?"

Logan smirked, "Whisky and beer sure, women? Well, there's only one woman I'm looking forward to seeing."

Paddy snorted at that sentiment, "Course ye are. And she's waiting for ye to get yer ass home. Come on, let's get on that plane."

"Yeah let's load up and get outta here." Logan and Paddy filed onto the plane with the rest of the Seabees, taking a seat behind the wings. The pilot came over the intercom and reminded everyone that they were leaving Iraq, and to hold onto their asses. The plane roared to life, screaming down the short runway. Cheers resounded through the plane as they became airborne.

The plane banked hard to the left, Logan felt tightness in his chest, struggling to bring his hand to his chest. Logan and Paddy glanced across the aisle, seeing an Equipment Operator attempting to puke in a Gatorade bottle. Logan winced at seeing the Senior Chief puking, as the plane banked into another combat maneuver.

"Jesus fuck!" Logan gritted through his teeth, feeling his own gut roll.

"Lord's name brother!" Paddy chastised Logan, chuckling at the misfortune of the higher ranking Chief puking.

It was night when they landed in Kuwait, Logan jogged for the phone bank to give Ann a call. He held his breath as the call connected, Ann's phone continued to ring. Before her voicemail connected, Logan's phone card notified him that he was out of time. The line went dead in his ear as he slammed the phone down on the receiver.

"Goddamn it!" Logan fumed as he heard the call to load the plane up for the second time. Running for the line waiting to get back on the flight, Logan spied Paddy in the herd. Pushing up through the crowd, he stood next to Paddy, who handed Logan a Monster.

"Ye look tense Logan. Everything okay?" Paddy was concerned for Logan, seeing a vein throbbing in his neck. The younger man was clearly pissed off about something, which made Paddy concerned for his brother.

"Tried to call Ann, my fucking phone card ran out." Logan griped as they found two seats near the back for the longest portion of the ride into London.

"Well when we land again, I'll loan ye mine. Ain't no one important as her that I need to call." Both men laughed at that thought, even though Paddy wished he had someone to call back home.

Paddy reached into the thigh pocket of his cammies, "Oh hey, I forgot I had this for ye. It came when ye was still in the hospital and I found it on me desk when I was packing up. Sorry brother."

Logan's took the outstretched piece of paper. He knew Ann's handwriting anywhere, even on the beat up, stained envelope. Flipping it over, Logan smirked at the words scrawled in big block letters:

'I JUST MISS YOU SO MUCH'

He tucked the letter into the pocket of his cammies; there was no need for him to read it since he would be seeing Ann in less than 48 hours. He could just ask her about it then. Right now, all he wanted was some sleep, especially since they would be stuck on the plane for the next seven hours nonstop.

Back in the States

Ann had gotten up while it was still dark, doing the final check through her bag and getting a shower before she drove down to JFK. Ann's nerves worked up on the drive down, but seeing the sun break over the horizon brought a serene calm to her nerves. She took a breath realizing that in less than 48 hours she would be standing on the flight line waiting to meet Logan for the first time.

Logan had made arrangements via email with the command ombudsman and the Chaplain for Ann to be on the flight line as his guest. He had put Ann in touch with Amy Kelly, the command ombudsman, who had called Ann personally with the details of the homecoming and mailed her the documents she would need to gain visitor access on the base. It had been a time consuming process; but after almost nine months of devoting time out of her life for Logan, there was no way she was missing finally meeting him in person. Ann had flown out to Los Angeles, picked up a rental and drove into Oxnard the day before the expected arrival date of Logan's flight.

Checking into the suite at the Embassy Suites Mandalay Beach (that Logan had graciously booked for the weekend of her stay) was a shock to Ann's jet lagged system. Walking into the hotel Ann was taken aback; the lobby was done in marble, crystal chandeliers hung from the gilded ceiling and the arching staircase straight out of Gone with the Wind made her realize this was no cheap place to stay. The front desk staff was extremely friendly and helpful; aware from Ann's driver's license she was not local.

"Welcome to the Embassy Mandalay Beach Ms. Stranahan. I'm sure you're tired from your flight; there is a reception out on the deck and dining in the restaurant if you're hungry. I see you've been reserved a king suite, there is a garden whirlpool tub for your enjoyment. You're in the west wing, beachfront third floor room 309. If there is anything I can do to help you enjoy your stay, by all means ring down." The receptionist didn't ask Ann for her credit card, which clued in that Logan had it all covered.

Walking around the spacious four room suite, Ann opened the windows and patio door stepping out onto the large balcony. A small table with two chairs and a palm tree were the only pieces of furniture on the balcony. The gorgeous view of the Pacific Ocean stole Ann's breath away; she had never seen the ocean, the salty breeze warming her skin. She never thought California to be this beautiful, always assuming that it was nothing but large cities that ran together. This view made that assumption completely invalid by far, even though she had drove through Los Angeles to get to Oxnard.

A knock startled Ann out of her moment of solace, "Just a minute!" she called running for the room's door.

A beautiful blonde woman about her age stood at the door with a large case at her feet, bag slung over her shoulder. "Ms. Stranahan? I'm Mindy, the onsite massage therapist that's been scheduled for you for the next two hours. Can I come in?"

Ann's jaw just dropped at that point, a massage therapist for her? For two hours? That would cost hundreds of dollars in New York! Ann stepped aside to let Mindy in the room, realizing the case at her feet was a portable massage table.

"Would you like to go out onto the balcony? The weather is absolutely beautiful today. It's very relaxing out on the Oceanside." Mindy definitely had the "Cali girl" accent, which made Ann smile.

"Um, yeah, sure, the balcony sounds great. Is there anything I need to do to get ready?" Ann had never had a massage before, so she wasn't sure of what were the normal procedures to getting one.

"Great! I'll get set up out there and all you need to do is come out in a towel. I'll make sure that you're covered up with a sheet. Take your time."

Two hours of chatting with Mindy while getting massaged was the best way for Ann to start relaxing after the nearly six hour nonstop flight. Mindy let Ann in on a lot of insider local info about the area, wishing her well with her Seabee coming home before heading out the door. After Mindy left, Ann filled the huge whirlpool tub; it was more than big enough for her and Logan both to relax in together. The hot water felt remarkable with her muscles relaxed from the massage. Ann inhaled and exhaled deeply, savoring the citrus scent of the soaking tablets.

Dressed in shorts and a t-shirt to wander down to the hotel's restaurant, her stomach reminded her that the last time she had ate was breakfast at JFK, almost twelve hours ago. Sitting down in the airy beachside dining room; Ann ordered a glass of wine, watching the waves lap gently at the shore before her dinner arrived.

She couldn't sleep that night in the king size bed; there was too much empty space, making Ann feel even more alone than she was. Slipping the worn soft brown t-shirt Logan had sent her over her bare skin; she stepped out onto the balcony. Logan's scent had long left the material, Ann usually slept in the conforming shirt when it wasn't in the laundry.

Leaning against the warm stone of the balcony, Ann whispered to the stars what was in her heart. The night would keep her secrets, helping to calm her nerves. The cool breeze licked at the edges of the shirt, the material caressing her bare thighs like an old lover.

"I know you're out there Logan looking at this same sky through the windows of a plane somewhere. I can't wait to see you and touch you. It's only a few more hours, and you'll really be real for me. These last nine months haven't been easy, but it's helped me realize that my heart belongs with you. You've been in my thoughts and prayers every day, and soon it will all be over. You'll be here, we'll be together finally." Silent tears slipped down Ann's cheeks, she wiped them away with her fingertips before going back inside to curl herself around one of the pillows in the bed.

After all they had been through since that fateful first box and letter, all the tears and heartache was coming to a close. Ann should be ecstatic to be seeing the man she loved for the first time, but she couldn't help the shreds of apprehension that lingered in her gut. Hopefully the morning light would burn those feelings away, and Ann could enjoy this weekend with Logan.

Chapter Twenty Three

London, United Kingdom

Logan took a long pull off the beer sitting in front of him in the bar in London. Paddy sat next to him, nursing a headache and a Guinness. They had fallen asleep on the flight, Paddy had slept with his head up against the window of the plane, cricked at an odd angle. Doc Ingram sat down between the boys, her tired eyes taking in the sight of the brothers looking a bit worse for wear.

"You boys look like you need something other than beers right now." Caitlin Ingram scooted two packs of ibuprofen across the bar, both men snatching the packs and choking the pills down with beer.

"Thanks love, we sure appreciate yer hospitality." Paddy grinned at the Corpsman, who patted him on the shoulder as she finished up her Crown and Coke.

"Don't mention it. Making this trip beats the hell out of everyone, I'm just making the rounds to my favorite people." Caitlin winked at Paddy before nodding to Logan as she left the boys at the bar.

Paddy and Logan turned to watch Ingram walk away, Paddy's eyes trained on the sway of her hips. Logan watched as Paddy stared, the flat of his hand connecting with Paddy's chest.

"Damn it brother! Can't a man appreciate a fine looking woman like that?" Paddy rubbed the aching space on his chest wincing at Logan.

"Yeah you can, but you ain't got to eye fuck her," Logan admonished. He had a lot of respect for Doc Ingram, especially since she had saved his life not but three weeks ago.

"Aye. Well, let's get ye to a phone so ye can call Ann. I'm sure she's dying to hear from ye." Paddy tossed back the last of his beer, clapping Logan on the shoulder as they stumbled out of the bar in search of a phone. Logan knew Ann was in Cali waiting on him, time was coming so quickly now. There would be another eleven hours to fly across the pond and most of the United States before they would land in Point Mugu.

He couldn't lie and say he wasn't nervous as hell to meet her, but he wouldn't let anyone know it either. Ann was the sole thought on his mind, nothing else mattered at the moment.

Oxnard, California

Soft light filtering through the bedroom woke Ann up from her deep sleep. It took a few seconds of looking around to remind herself that she was in a hotel room in California and that in just a few hours Logan would be stepping off a plane from Kuwait. Ann knew they would be flying into Kuwait and then flying into Point Mugu. Amy had been a godsend over the last month helping Ann to understand what was going to happen the last few weeks of the deployment by phone and email from Colorado.

Ann took her time eating breakfast, brought by room service, on the balcony. The warm breeze blowing in off the ocean warmed her skin, as her hair flowed down her shoulders gracefully. Sipping her orange juice, Ann noticed a missed call on her phone. Bringing up her voicemail and hitting the speakerphone while eating, her heart skipped a beat when Logan's timbre filled the quiet of the balcony.

"Hey sweetheart, I know you're probably sleeping as it's something like," she could hear him shuffling around to look at his watch, "five in the morning in Cali. I hope you liked the massage and the room. We're getting ready to leave London shortly. I'll be seeing you for dinner. Can't wait to see you on the flight line. Don't forget to get with Amy today to get your sponsorship onto base. Sleep tight, goodnight." His voice sounded tired but excited to Ann's ears, she could tell he was excited to see her in his own way.

Ann spent the better part of the morning texting back and forth with Amy, trying to calm her nerves. Amy had done this plenty of times, her husband Sean was the Commanding Officer of NMCB 17. Amy suggested a shopping trip with her out to Thousand Oaks Mall, to get their mind off the men coming home later in the afternoon.

The two women had gotten their hair done, picked out shoes and dresses, topping the afternoon off with a delicious sushi lunch. It was nice to spend the afternoon before the boys pulled in with someone Ann considered friend. Amy had known exactly how to get Ann calmed down with the girl's afternoon out. The officer's wife refused to let Ann pay for anything, knowing she was in medical school and living on a limited income.

"Darlin', Sean makes more than enough for me to spoil you a bit. You ain't gotta worry about paying me back, consider it a gift." Amy's western drawl filled the space of Amy's car when Ann offered to pay her back. The younger girl blushed and accepted the gift, knowing Logan would like seeing her all dolled up. Amy dropped Ann off at her hotel, promising to meet her at the front gate of the base in a couple of hours.

Ann stood on the flight line of Point Mugu Naval Air Station in a just above the knee length floral summer dress and wedge sandals. Her hair hung loose over her shoulders, the golden tendrils swaying in the coastal California breeze. Around her stood young wives holding nearly new babies to their chests; older women with young children dressed in their best holding signs for their daddy's, welcoming them home from deployment. Ann couldn't imagine the struggle being pregnant with her man gone to war, or explaining to little ones that daddy would be coming home from work soon more than once when a nightmare woke them in tears.

The military jet taxied up to the tarmac; the crowd erupted into cheers, drowning out the dying engines of the plane. Ann felt those butterflies return to her belly that she had been fighting since getting into Cali yesterday. Amy stood next to Ann, explaining that the winner of the first kiss lottery got to disembark first, new dads next, it would go officers after new dads and then by work center. Amy assured her that CM's wouldn't be too far from the front of the plane, so Ann wouldn't be waiting long for Logan.

Seeing all the new dads crying meeting their babies for the first time tugged at Ann's emotions. She was happy for these families to have their hero home after being gone so long. Amy paired off shortly after, seeing her husband Sean in the herd coming off from the plane. Amy had kissed Ann on the cheek, assuring her it would be fine meeting Logan and that she looked great. Ann watched with tears in her eyes as Amy ran up to her husband, Sean enveloping his wife into his arms as they greeted each other.

Ann never realized the emotion involved in the pictures and videos she had seen online of service members when they came home from deployment. She had never met her brother when he had come home from deployment, he'd never wanted the family to take away from the work to be done on the farm. Ann was always glad to see him when he did come home from deployment, except for the last time.

Ann watched more of the Seabees meeting up with family members, while others piled onto a bus that didn't have family waiting for them. The Seabees really all started looking the same-- wearing the same uniforms and carrying backpacks. It was a few minutes after Amy left her that Ann saw what could pass for a model of a handsome man with stunning blue eyes, playfully elbow the man with rugged good looks walking alongside him carrying a single lavender rose in his hand. The first man pointed at Ann, whose heart began to hammer in her chest when she recognized it was Logan carrying the rose in his hand. Recognition hit Logan; handing his backpack off to the guy he stood with.

Ann took off at a run, her legs wrapping around Logan's waist as she jumped into his arms. Logan pulled Ann up against his chest; she fit so right against him, his arms around her back pulling her close. She smelled just as he remembered her smelling, her skin soft against his calloused fingertips.

Ann pressed her lips to Logan's in a long awaited heated kiss that took both their breath away. Pulling away she laid her head in the slope of Logan's neck and shoulder, crying in earnest, as Logan held her to his chest. Ann breathed in deep of the scent she knew was his, masculine, strong, every bit Logan. In his arms she felt safe, in his arms she was home.

"Hey baby, I'm home." Logan drawled against Ann's neck, his lips caressing her pulse point, making Ann shiver against him. Those were the sweetest words Ann had heard in a long,

long time. She nodded against his neck, tears slipping inside his uniform blouse. Logan was home, this was real, and he was *finally* real. Everything they had worked through, survived through was now behind them. In this moment it was only them, nothing else mattered. Logan didn't want to let Ann go, but he knew they couldn't stand there forever.

Logan carefully set Ann down, keeping her pulled to his chest as he kissed her hair. Ann sniffled against his chest, carefully wiping her eyes. She could feel and hear Logan's nervous chuckle as he held her, running his fingertips along her spine. Nervous energy filled both of them, Ann could feel the twinges of desire filling low in her abdomen.

"You better now baby doll?" Logan's deep blue eyes searched Ann's face, concern written all over his features. He'd never had anyone waiting for him on the flight line; this was all as new for him as it was for Ann. He wasn't so sure of the feelings surging inside him, so many emotions rolling over him at once. The fear had burned away the moment she ran into his arms, what was replacing it was happiness and desire for the woman against his chest. This woman loved him as much as he loved her, it was crazy to think that nine months ago they were strangers. That one fateful care package ignited the spark that fed the flames of the relationship they had now.

"Yeah, I'm just so glad to finally be able to meet you. I didn't mean to cry, I'm just so happy." Ann's voice was a choppy whisper as she took the rose from Logan's hand, holding it close to her chest. He'd brought her a lavender rose, Ann smiled at the sentiment behind the beautiful color. It didn't matter if he was aware of it, what mattered was that he had thought to give it to her.

Logan tucked a stray lock of hair behind Ann's ear, brushing his lips against hers tenderly. Ann sighed contentedly, as a smirk came across his lips. He was glad to be home, glad to be with her. He wiped the tears from her eyes with his thumb, not wanting to break contact with her.

"You look amazing Ann. I'm so glad you could make it out to meet me. You ready to go? I really want a shower and some dinner." The grin on his face made Ann melt; this was a man who was truly happy to be home.

"This must be the infamous Ann Stranahan. Aye lass, yer more beautiful in the flesh than yer picture." Paddy's eyes took in the tender scene in front of him, he was genuinely happy for his brother finally getting to meet his woman in person.

Ann giggled at the man addressing her, knowing who it was immediately by the accent. There were so many things she wanted to say to Paddy, but every one of those things slipped out the window. Ann wriggled out of Logan's grip, stepping over to the Irishman and wrapping her arms around his slim waist.

Paddy ran his hand over the top of Ann's head, her cheek resting against his chest. The young woman was so small compared to him and Logan; she fit easily in his side. That was where Ann belonged, protected in Logan's side.

"Thank you Paddy, for everything." Ann looked up into the Irishman's infectious smile. Thanking him was the least of what she could say to him in that moment.

"Yer welcome love, anything for ye and me brother. Ye need anything, ye give me a call eh? He ever gets too big for his britches ye let me know love, I'll put him in his place!" Paddy winked conspiratorially at Ann before Logan grumbled, taking Ann by the hand and grabbing his backpack.

"Come on. Let's go get my truck out of destroyed parking so we can return your rental." Logan wrapped his fingers around Ann's, leading her and Paddy towards visitor parking.

At this moment, his world was now complete, the sands of Iraq behind him. It was the beginning of a new chapter in his life with the woman he loved beside him.

Chapter Twenty Four

Ann climbed up in the passenger side of Logan's truck after handing off the keys to her rental to Paddy. She was glad there were running boards along the sides of the big four wheel drive; it wouldn't have been very lady like of her to jump up in there with the dress on. Logan probably would have appreciated the sight of her panties, but that wasn't something Paddy needed to see.

Ann scooted over to the middle of the seat; Logan draping his arm over her shoulders to pull her close against him as they drove through the base, Paddy following close behind. Logan knew where the rental needed returned to in Oxnard. With the rental returned, Ann found herself sitting between Paddy and Logan in the truck as they headed back onto base to drop Paddy off at the barracks and to pick up Logan's sea bag.

Stopping outside the Seabee barracks, Ann slid carefully to the edge of the truck seat, taking Logan's hand to be helped out. She didn't realize that he would swing her out of the driver's seat and flush against his chest. The gesture looked innocent to anyone observing from the outside, but the tension between Logan and Ann was more than palpable.

Electricity crackled between them, Logan's stormy eyes settled on the chain around Ann's neck, his fingers running through the chain, brushing against her skin. Ann shivered at the touch, knowing that while on base there would be no display of public affection between them. What little bit was shown on the flight line was acceptable, Logan had just returned home. But holding hands, kissing or anything else was frowned upon. That was just how the regulations were; there was nothing Ann could do about it.

Paddy came around the side of the truck, dropping Logan's sea bag into the bed before coming to say goodbye to his brother. His gaze fell to the two people standing close, Logan's fingers on Ann's skin. Paddy could see the tension between them, they needed time alone. The emotions between them were so heavy he could feel it pulling inside his own chest.

"Aye, got yer bag in the truck. Thanks fer the ride back here. If ye ain't got plans tomorrow night, I'd love to hang with ye." Paddy coughed, kicking at the concrete with the toe of his boot, feeling like a voyeur seeing this intimate moment between the two lovers.

Logan released his hold on the petite blonde in his arms, walking over to grip the outstretched hand. "Thanks brother. Couldn'ta done this deployment without you. Here's my number, give me a holler tomorrow when you're ready to get outta here. We'll toss some back."

"Will do. I'll pick up a new phone from the NEX. Got nothing but time to kill tonight. Ye take care of that beautiful lass ye hear?" Paddy pulled Logan into a hug, feeling the other man's arms tighten around his back. This was a bond forged in the fires of war, a bond that would last a lifetime.

"I will. I promise you that." Logan released the older man, smirking at the memory of Paddy's earlier comment about kicking his ass if he misbehaved towards Ann. That wasn't just a joke; those words were more truth than fiction. Paddy would kick Logan's ass across the base and back again if he mistreated Ann, not that Logan ever would.

Paddy brought Ann into his chest, kissing the top of her head. He could feel the tension inside her small frame; he couldn't imagine the emotions welling inside her.

"It'll be okay love, he's a good guy. Just take it slow tonight eh? No one's forcing ye to do anything ye don't want to hmm?" His murmured brogue must have brought comfort to Ann, her body slumped against him.

"Thanks Paddy. I'm sure it will be okay, just so much emotion built up after so much time." Ann couldn't help but voice her fears to this man she barely knew, but somehow knew she could trust without question.

Paddy looked over Ann's shoulder, seeing Logan packing his lip from a can of Copenhagen he'd pulled out of his blouse pocket. Logan had the same nervous habit, nicotine. While it wasn't smoking like Paddy, it still was the fix that Logan needed to calm his nerves. Paddy grinned, knowing that before long they both would settle down and be okay around each other. It would be finding that comfortable ground that would be difficult.

"I understand love. I have yer number, when I get me phone tonight I'll text ye me number. If ye need me, text or call. I'll answer for ye, no matter what time. Doubt either of us will sleep much with the time change." Paddy kissed Ann on the forehead, gently turning her towards Logan with a playful smack on her bottom.

"Ya gonna let go of my girlfriend anytime soon there Irish? Or am I gonna have to come kick your ass?" Logan called over, feigning pissed off.

"Fuck ye Dixon. She likes me better anyways! She's all yers fer tonight!" Paddy laughed heartily, winking at Ann, whose face turned beet red at the playful banter between the two Chief's.

Ann turned back to look at Paddy one last time as Logan helped her into the truck, the look on her face was strained. Paddy nodded his head, a slight grin painting his features. Ann smiled, waving slightly before climbing the rest of the way into the truck.

Paddy waved to Logan as the truck pulled out of the barracks parking lot. He knew then that things would be okay, Logan and Ann had waited too long for this; they just needed time to adjust to being physically together.

Checking into his barracks room and dropping off his luggage didn't take Paddy long at all. As much as he wanted a shower, food and sleep, a new phone got the better of him. Paddy lit up a smoke as he walked through the base, heading towards the Navy Exchange. There was nothing wrong with picking up a bottle of Jameson and a fresh pack of smokes after dinner. Once he had his new phone set up, Paddy planned on a shower before hanging out on the quiet on his balcony and relaxing with a nice drink. After the hell he had experienced, he was entitled to a little downtime.

Chapter Twenty Five

Ann led Logan through the hotel to the elevator, amid cheers of "Welcome home Chief!" and "Bravo Zulu Seabee!" with people clapping. Logan couldn't remember the last time people had made such a fuss over him coming home, but he couldn't deny it felt good. Ann's hand was enveloped in Logan's; her face red as he waved and smiled politely to the people around them.

"Does this always happen when you come home?" Ann breathed a sigh of relief when they were in the silence of the glass elevator, looking out over the grounds of the resort.

"No. This is the first time anyone's ever met me on the flight line, much less spent a weekend with me. I've never had this many people thank me and wish me well on being home." Logan touched Ann's arm, bringing her focus around to him.

Ann looked up at him, stretching up to press her lips to his, only to have Logan turn away from her. The sting of rejection bit at her heart, she never thought it would be like this—that Logan would swing from wanting her to pushing her away so quickly.

Logan noticed the hurt in her eyes, running his fingers over her cheek to focus her gaze on his face. He tapped his bottom lip and chin gently, bringing her attention to him.

"Sorry darlin' I got shit in my lip. Ain't gonna kiss you with it in. Nothing personal, nothing wrong with you. Just don't want you experiencing that." Logan chuckled at seeing Ann visibly relax. It really wasn't anything against her; he just didn't want her tasting Copenhagen on his lips, much less getting a mouthful of the gritty tobacco if she decided to deepen the kiss. He wasn't that much of a dick; even though other women he knew didn't care, Ann was something special.

The elevator dinged on the third floor, breaking the moment between them. Ann stepped out into the vacant hallway, turning left as Logan followed alongside her. She could feel her heart start to beat quicker as they neared the room; she hoped her palms weren't sweating.

Logan stood behind Ann as she fiddled with her purse to get the room key out. He could tell she was nervous, her hand shook just enough for him to notice as the key slid into the lock. He readjusted his gear bag on his shoulder, giving her a bit more room. Ann opened the door to the spacious room, immediately tossing her purse onto the table and kicking off her shoes.

She moaned at the feel of carpet under her toes, her feet hurt from standing in the wedges on the tarmac for most of the afternoon. Ann didn't know how women wore heels all day long without their feet and legs killing them.

She was glad to be in a profession that heels were not a requirement.

Turning around to look at Logan, she noticed he had set his backpack down on the table, with his duffle bag still over his shoulder. He was watching her as much as she was watching him, neither of them knowing the next move to make.

Logan swallowed thickly, "I'm gonna go get a shower and all. That way we can head out to dinner. Just be a bit." He headed off towards the bedroom, making a beeline for the double sized bathroom.

Ann couldn't help but gawk watching Logan walk away. Something about the raw masculinity of the man made her insides quiver. She heard the shower come on minutes later, her thoughts drifted to the not so clean kind. Logan had probably turned the water on to warm up while he was stripping down.

Here the man was; mere feet away from her in a shower, wet and naked and she was standing in the middle of the bedroom staring at the door. Had it been any other woman, anyone but Ann, they would have probably joined Logan in that shower. But that didn't seem right to her, he still needed his space and his privacy.

Ann stepped out onto the balcony, watching the waves crash against the shore. Her thoughts circled back to every letter, email, phone call and Skype conversation they had over the last nine months. There was nothing they didn't really know about each other, or couldn't figure out. Why was being with him now, in person, so very hard?

Logan looked out across the hotel room as he buttoned his jeans and buckled his belt. Seeing the breeze blowing through Ann's golden hair on the balcony made his heart race, he couldn't understand how a beautiful woman like her could be in love with an ugly mug like him. Even still, he thanked his lucky stars as he pulled on his well-worn buckaroo boots and stepped out onto the balcony. He felt more like himself in his own clothes, rather than the Chief she knew him as. Maybe seeing him comfortable would help break the ice?

Logan reached out, running his fingertips over Ann's uncovered arms. She shivered at his touch; but didn't balk. Wrapping his arms around her shoulders, Ann leaned into his strength, taking comfort in his lean body touching hers.

"You ready to get some dinner? Heard the restaurant downstairs is pretty good." His breath tickled her neck, Ann nodded acknowledging his presence fully.

"I could eat. Do you care if I wear my flip flops? Those wedges kill." Ann could feel Logan's chest vibrating, the chuckle low in his throat.

"Sweetheart, whatever makes you comfortable. You can go barefoot for all I care. Come on." Logan felt Ann twist in his grip, her sky blue hues searching his face as if she was looking at him with new eyes.

"Mmh, you smell nice. Look a bit different outside the uniform too. I wouldn't have thought you the cowboy type though with the tattoos." Ann's lips turned up in a smile, Logan's hands settled on her hips.

"Well I didn't figure you to be so much more beautiful in person. Guess we surprised each other huh?" Logan brought Ann's lips to his, his tongue parting them gently as he sought purchase within her.

Ann sighed, her body melding into Logan's her palms flat on his chest, as he kissed her tenderly. This man, something about him that she couldn't put a finger on, made her turn to mush.

She could feel the heat of the kiss running down her spine, pooling in between her thighs. Sparks twinkled behind her eyelids as her pulse quickened. Ann struggled to control her breathing, but it was a losing battle.

Thoughts filled Ann's mind of running her nails over the cross tattoo that ran the length of Logan's ribs, her body shivered with a moan escaping into Logan's mouth.

Logan pulled away, running his knuckles over her cheek. "Babygirl, we ain't gotta go anywhere if you don't want to. We could order room service in and stay up here if you want." The words came out in his husky drawl; Ann knew his thoughts were the same place hers were, but that didn't mean that they had to act on them.

"Be a shame that you got all cleaned up and dressed up to just get naked and dirty again." Ann snickered, seeing Logan's eyes light up with an evil grin crossing his rugged features.

"Darlin' for you, I'd do anything you wanted. Food sounds like a good plan though." Logan subtly stretched his hip, adjusting the tightness in his jeans. This woman in his arms made him burn with desire, something no other woman he had been with had done. As much as he wanted her, he knew his body needed food, especially since the last time he had ate had been over twelve hours before in London.

The look on Ann's face made him bust out laughing, if looks could have killed he would have been dead right there.

"Logan Dixon! You have got to be kidding me!" Ann couldn't hide the miffed look on her face, but then again she didn't know when the last time he had ate a meal had been. His body was probably running on fumes and she had lunch with Amy not six hours prior, it would benefit them both to eat a meal. Especially if the kiss they just shared held any promise for later in the evening.

"No ma'am. Last time I ate was London about twelve hours ago. Come on, let's grab some dinner. We got the whole weekend to get to know each other better. Thank God you don't know my middle name." Logan laughed as he opened the door to the hotel room, Ann sneaking out under his arm into the hallway. He watched as that dress sashayed around her hips and thighs, that woman was going to be the death of him before the weekend was over.

Chapter Twenty Six

Ann pulled her legs up underneath her as they ate dinner. The salmon and steak was forgotten as the wine and whisky helped to calm the nerves between her and Logan. Ann laughed as Logan regaled her with the jokes that flew around the galley when her first box arrived. They sat on the patio eating, laughing and enjoying each other's company until the Pacific sky started to turn a beautiful shade of pink.

Logan paid the bill, watching Ann walk towards the beach. The ocean was calling both of their names with its siren song. Ann kicked off her sandals, watching Logan sit on the hotel property wall to remove his boots and roll up his jeans. Her hand fit easily in his as they walked through the warm sand, the grains massaging their feet and toes as they found a quiet spot down the beach from the hotel.

Logan pulled Ann to his chest, wrapping his arms around her knees, sharing his body heat with her. Ann laid back against him, her head resting on his shoulder as she sighed contentedly.

"Mhm Logan, I don't think this night could be any more perfect." She heard a resounding agreement hum in his chest, his lips tracing the artery in her neck.

"It's been a good night for sure." Logan let the silence linger between them as the sun started to set, the air turning cooler as he pulled Ann up from the sand.

"Let's head on back. That breeze can get awful damn cold at night. I've stood out in it plenty in formations and froze my ass off."

By the time they made it up to the room they were a breathless, laughing, pawing mess. Ann skirted around Logan at the door, heading off for the bathroom. He heard the water in the overlarge tub come on, his brain immediately going to Ann shimmying out of that dress to pool on the bathroom floor. He stalked her like prey, finding her bent over the tub testing the water temperature as she tossed in scented bath soap.

Logan ran his fingertips up Ann's soft thighs, pushing the hem of her dress up over her hips. Hooking his fingers in her barely there panties, running them down her slim legs without protest from her. Ann shivered, feeling Logan's fingers trail down her neck, unzipping the dress that pooled around her feet.

Ann turned around to see the fire ignite in Logan's eyes, her breath catching in her throat. She'd never seen fire like that in anyone's eyes when they looked at her.

If Logan could have fell to his knees and worshipped the woman standing naked in front of him he would have. Ann's smooth skin was unmarred by scar or tattoo, so much different than he was used to, that was what hooked him.

Ann stepped into the tub, the water covering the swells of her breasts as she swirled the water around her. A smirk crossed her lips as she crooked her finger at him.

"You coming Logan?" Ann quirked her eyebrow at him, eyeing him mischievously. She turned from him to fiddle with the water level and the jets as he quickly undressed.

Running a hand over his face, Logan unbuckled his belt, popping the top button to fight the dress shirt free from the snug Wrangler jeans. Logan's fingers sped through the buttons as he wrestled the shirt to the bathroom floor on top of Ann's dress. He stepped out of the jeans, the bulge of his erection pressing against the rigid denim painfully.

"Ain't gotta ask me twice babygirl."
Logan stepped into the tub, the hot water
making his skin tingle as he sat down near
Ann, his fingers running over her
collarbones, cupping her breasts in his
hands. A choked moan escaped Ann's lips,
feeling his roughened hands skate over
her skin.

The palms of Ann's hands rested on
the hard planes of Logan's chest; her
fingernails grazing the ridges as she
became familiar with the man she had
fallen in love with. Logan's tongue found
purchase between Ann's lips; she accepted
his intrusion without question. The sigh
Ann emitted made him grin against her
mouth, his thoughts turning back to the
same ones he had in the shower in Iraq.

Ann's fingers stuttered to a halt
when the deep ridge of a scar on Logan's
ribcage passed through her touch. Ann
jerked away from Logan, his eyes
mirroring the hurt she was sure was in her
own.

Logan locked eyes with Ann; seeing the emotions swirling within her, the hurt, the fear, the anger of knowing that he was wounded. Ann remembered feeling helpless to do anything to help Logan when he was injured. The only lifeline she had to him was through Paddy, who called her as soon as he knew anything, assuring her that Logan was going to be fine.

"Baby, I promise you I'm fine. I'm here with you, a whole man. It could have been worse, luckily it wasn't. I'm here now, with you and that's all that matters." Logan reached out, wiping the tears streaking down Ann's face with his thumb before kissing her gently. "What matters is here, now and us. The past is over and gone. We go forward from here okay?"

Ann nodded; a breath blustering out from her burning lungs, her head laid on Logan's shoulder as words whispered into his ear. "I was just so scared for you. I swear I kept my phone with me everywhere I went those first few days

waiting to hear from Paddy. He was a
godsend keeping me sane."

"Paddy's a good guy. He's my
brother, maybe not by blood, but by
choice. He's a better brother than Butch
ever was." Logan ran his wet fingers
through Ann's hair, savoring the feel of the
soft strands gliding between his digits.

Logan's hands dipped beneath the
steamy water, coming to rest on Ann's
slender hips. He trailed his fingers over
her abdomen, finding the apex of her
thighs. Ann's thighs parted, giving Logan
access to her most intimate flesh. Pressing
on slowly, Logan chuckled at the gasp that
escaped Ann when the pad of his
forefinger came in contact with the bundle
of nerves before dipping inside her.

Working slowly as to not cause Ann
pain, Logan stroked her inner walls with a
steady rhythm he was sure would bring
her release. Ann moaned in appreciation
at the touch, her blood starting to boil as

hormones raced through her weary system.

"Please Logan," Ann mumbled against his neck, her fingers digging into his shoulders.

"Please what sweetheart?" Logan couldn't keep the grin off his face; he knew exactly what she was asking for, but he wanted to hear it from her. He knew she had a dirty girl hidden down deep, phone calls and Skype had proved that during the deployment. The difference now was that they were in the same place at the same time, not separated by a computer screen or a phone line that was sometimes iffy.

"Please make me come." Ann knew he could do it, he'd proven it just by talking to her on the phone. That was words, this was actions. She needed to feel him make her come, to know he was really with her, to prove to herself he was whole.

Logan growled his assent, his fingers keeping their steady pace as the fingers of his other hand came into play, caressing the tight bundle of nerves. He could feel the nips and kisses along his neck, the touch of her mouth on his skin enticing him to push her farther, he needed to see her come undone.

Ann felt the burn low in her belly; her legs began to tremble as her breaths became shorter. Logan was playing her like a well–tuned instrument, one he knew better than she thought he did.

Logan grunted when Ann's teeth bit into his skin; a low guttural moan swelled from her throat, as she gripped his fingers tight within her. Shivers wracked her slim frame, the water still hot around them. Logan pulled Ann against his chest, kissing her as he caressed her face.

"You better now sweetheart?" Logan's pulse thrummed through his veins, he hungered to be inside Ann more than anything. But seeing her eyes fluttering shut reminded him of how long she had been awake at this point—it wouldn't be fair to keep her up any longer. Logan blew out a calming breath, standing up to step out of the tub.

Ann's heart dropped when she saw the aching hard-on that Logan was trying to ignore. He'd made her come, gave her the release she had been waiting nine months for without asking for anything in return. She felt guilty, reaching out to catch his hand before he grabbed the towels.

"Logan, let me take care of you." Ann's plea fell on deaf ears as Logan shook his head, helping her out of the tub and wrapping a towel around her.

"Nah. You're tired. I'm good. I'm not tired. Let's get you dried off and into bed. We have plenty of time to take care of me. Come on." Logan led Ann into the bedroom, sitting her down on the bed. Ann watched Logan dig through his bag, pulling a pair of sleep pants up over his ass and hips.

Logan helped Ann dry off before turning down the blankets on the bed. He made sure she was comfortable, laying a chaste kiss on her lips.

"I'm not going anywhere. I'm just gonna go watch some TV in the other room. You get some rest, there's still plenty of the weekend left." His murmured words hummed against Ann's frown, Logan knew she wasn't happy with him.

"Are you going to come to bed eventually?" Ann questioned, not liking the prospect of sleeping alone after waiting so long to finally be with him.

Exasperated, Logan forced a smile. "Eventually. I'm still on Iraq time babe. I promise you won't sleep alone tonight. Sleep well."

Ann watched Logan walk out of the dark bedroom, hearing the ominous click of the door slowly closing behind him. She waited until she heard the TV come on and the volume lower before reaching for her cellphone on the night stand next to her.

A text message with an 847 number was on the screen, taking her thoughts to another part of the city and another man she loved. Ann knew he would be awake just like Logan, time was his nemesis just as it was Logan's tonight.

Chapter Twenty Seven

Ann woke to the sheets tangled in her bare legs. Reaching across the bed she found Logan's side still somewhat made. Either he had come to bed and made his side when he woke up, or he had fallen asleep watching TV. Ann hedged her bets on the latter rather than the former.

Stretching as she rose from the bed, Ann felt her back and shoulders pop. She couldn't imagine how stiff Logan as from sleeping on the couch. It probably was more comfortable than his bed in Iraq, but it was still a couch. Sleeping on couches was never anything to be done for long term. Ann crept through the hotel room, not caring to put on clothes as it was early morning. It was just her and Logan in the room, clothes were the last thing on either of their minds. They had seen each other naked last night in the tub, what was the point of clothes now? Modesty be damned as far as Ann was concerned.

Logan caught Ann's subtle scent on the breeze, as she joined him on the warm concrete of the patio. He felt guilty for falling asleep on the couch, and not going to bed with her. He wasn't tired, and he didn't want to keep Ann up tossing and turning in the bed.

He'd woke up to make a cup of coffee, taking up a chair on the balcony to watch the sun rise over the Pacific Ocean. This sunrise reminded him of the many he'd watched in the mornings in Iraq. Even in the hell of war, there was beauty.

Ann settled into Logan's lap, a knee settled beside each of his thighs, her gaze catching his as she took the cup of coffee from his hand. Logan smirked, watching Ann finish off the last dregs of his coffee, her nipples brushing against his chest.

"Morning." Ann smiled brightly, setting the now empty mug on the small breakfast table. She laced her arms around Logan's neck, pressing her lips to his in a passionate kiss.

Logan could taste coffee mixed with the mint of her toothpaste as Ann kissed him. Other parts of him started to respond to the close proximity of her body, pressing against her sitting in his lap.

"Mornin' darlin'" Logan drawled against Ann's lips, his hands caressing her spine. Ann moaned, the sound turning Logan on even more. He could feel himself straining against the thin fabric of his underwear to get closer to Ann's wet core.

Ann reached down between them, snaking her hands into the waistband of Logan's underwear, shimmying them down his hips just enough to free his length from the tight confines. She began stroking Logan in a lazy, stuttered motion, seeing the burn building in his eyes. Logan's head dropped onto her shoulder, his lips and teeth kissing and nipping at her neck. Ann could feel her own juices soaking through Logan's underwear, the feel of him in her hand mixed with the feelings of what he was doing to her was almost too much.

Ann gasped, rocking her hips to rub herself along Logan's hard length. The purely animalistic growl that escaped him made her shiver violently.

"Sweetheart, I've waited nine months for this. Can't hold back no longer." The words coming out a strangled plea from this strong man beneath her gave Ann courage that she had never known before. It turned her on to know Logan wanted her more than anything else, that he could barely restrain himself anymore.

Logan groaned at the feeling of Ann taking him within her. She was wet, warm and oh so tight. It had been a long time since he'd last been laid, he knew he wasn't going to last long. Not with this woman he loved completely rolling her hips against him. Ann gritted her teeth at the first few inches of Logan entering her, she had never been with anyone so well-endowed before. But once she stretched to accommodate, Ann was in heaven rolling her hips against Logan.

Logan tucked his head into Ann's chest, breathing in her scent, placing soft kisses against her breasts as her fingers threaded through his short cropped hair. He could feel the Channel Islands breeze blowing around them as Ann rode him in the chair on the balcony. Tendrils of her hair tickled his back as she moaned above him, her thighs trembling around his own.

Ann felt the slow burn of her orgasm building in her belly, feeling Logan bucking underneath her, charging towards his own release. This was what she wanted, this private moment between them that they could be one soul finally.

Logan glanced up, seeing Ann's eyes closed, her lips forming a sexy "o" that he couldn't help but want to kiss. Reaching up, he pulled Ann's head down to his, sucking her bottom lip in between his own. Ann groaned into his mouth, Logan felt her orgasm pulse through her, gripping him tight as it pulled his own orgasm from him.

Ann pulled from Logan's grip, kissing him tenderly on the mouth, as she stood to walk back into the hotel room.

"Mhm, that was amazing." The words were breathless and laced with passion. A morning orgasm was just what Ann needed to start her day, especially with what she had planned.

"Yeah, that was something else for sure. Good thing I ordered breakfast in. We need it after that." As if on cue a knock came at the door, to which Logan pulled his underwear up and casually answered. Ann was in shock as to how he thought nothing of answering the door in his underwear soaked with the product of their lovemaking, while she ran for the shower.

But that was what made them different. He had no filter, she had filter. They evened each other out, that was just the cornerstone of this now physical relationship they were adding onto their emotional relationship.

Ann showered in the master bathroom, while Logan showered in the bathroom off the living room. Breakfast was forgotten on the table as Ann braided her hair, watching Logan tuck his t-shirt into his jeans in the bedroom.

She was comfortable around him now, something she was sure would come the more she was physically around him. Sighing as she buttoned her shorts, Ann caught the scent of breakfast on the air. Logan was out in the small dining room, opening the dishes that room service had brought a short while ago.

Logan's stomach growled at the sight of bacon, pancakes and real eggs. None of that powdered shit that was served in the galley and was claimed to be eggs. These were honest to God real eggs!

Ann took a seat across from Logan, digging into the pancakes smothered in whipped cream and strawberries. Neither spoke as they ate, their thoughts were focused on the meal in front of them.

Logan set his fork down after the last bite of eggs, drinking deep from the glass of milk in front of him. The first few meals back in the states always tasted best after coming back from deployment.

"So what is it you have planned for today? I figured we could just fly by the seat of our pants and do whatever came to us." Logan watched as Ann took the last bite of bacon, chewing thoughtfully. Her expression didn't betray anything out of sorts, he wasn't worried about them doing anything he wouldn't like.

Ann swallowed her breakfast, choosing her next words carefully. She really wanted what she had planned to be a surprise. What was a surprise if you already knew what was going to happen?

"I thought we could hang out here at the hotel today. Swim and just lounge around. Since I have to fly back tomorrow evening, we only have about twenty four hours left together." Ann smiled brightly, hoping to send Logan off her track and into the brush.

"I guess we could do that. I was planning on taking you to the Seabee Museum, and maybe the NEX on base to pick up a few things. But we can always bump that to tomorrow before you fly out. Maybe grab some lunch at In and Out before I run you down to LAX."

Ann grinned, realizing she had accomplished her goal of getting Logan off the thought of what she had planned for the day. Hopefully the other people involved with the plan were on their way over and ready for the plans that were hatched last night via a long string of text messages.

Logan didn't know what Ann had up her sleeve, but she was determined to not give him an inch of knowing what it was. Fine, he'd let her have the secret. There was worse things the woman could come up with than playing in the pool or at the beach for the day.

Working together, they quickly cleaned up the dishes from breakfast before straightening up the hotel room. Logan took his dirty uniform out to his truck, tossing the offending article of clothing in the toolbox. He'd deal with it when he got back to Colorado on Tuesday. After dropping Ann off at LAX, he'd book a room at the Navy Lodge or bunk down with Paddy in the barracks for the last couple of nights in California.

His thoughts lingered to his house in Colorado, and how it would be empty now with Mels gone. He hated living alone, maybe if things worked out between him and Ann this weekend he could talk her into moving to Colorado next year when she finished school?

Ann nearly jumped out of her skin when Logan's lips grazed her neck, his fingers gripping into her hips as he pulled her close.

"You're insatiable you know that?" Ann muttered as Logan nipped her earlobe, his breath hot on the shell of her ear.

"What do you expect when we've danced this dance for the last nine months and I've got you all to myself for the weekend?" Logan pressed the front of his jeans into Ann's backside, his want of her clearly apparent.

Ann chuckled, "Well that's a sound thesis if I ever heard one." Turning in Logan's arms Ann leaned in to press a chaste kiss to his lips, running her nails over his tight t-shirt.

A solid knock came at the door, startling them both as Ann broke away to answer it. Logan watched Ann with hungry eyes as she skipped over to the door, her braid bouncing against her back as the muscles in her ass rippled under the denim shorts.

"Hello love! Didna interrupt anything did we?" Paddy pulled Ann into a crushing hug, looking over her shoulder and winking at Logan.

"Oh no, Logan and I weren't up to anything...yet. Good to see you Paddy. Oh! Who do you have with you?" Ann broke away from Paddy to turn her attention to the other person with him, who was skilfully hiding behind the Irishman.

"This, love, is Caitlin Ingram. She's the woman who saved yer man's life over in Iraq." Paddy pulled Caitlin into the hotel room as Ann enveloped the older woman into a tight hug, thanking her profusely.

This was Ann's surprise, Logan couldn't think of anyone else he'd rather spend the day with than his girlfriend, the woman who saved his life and his brother. This day was just getting better and better, and it was just getting started.

Chapter Twenty Eight

Logan laughed out loud as Caitlin came up sputtering for air from the bottom of the pool. She thought she would get the best of him by trying to pull his swim trunks off, failing in her attempt. Logan pushed her down to the bottom of the pool before letting her come up for air.

Caitlin pushed her hair out of her eyes, scowling at Logan. "Asshole! I almost had you!"

"Nah. You were far off from sneaking up on me. I heard you a long ways off." Logan patted the side of the Corpsman's cheek before he swam to the shallow end of the pool to see what Paddy and Ann were chatting animatedly about.

Caitlin followed Logan to the shallow end, lacing herself under Paddy's arm. His hand fell naturally onto her chest, fingers absently toying with the strap of her bikini top.

Ann felt the blush rise in her skin, she didn't feel comfortable wearing a two piece, no matter what Logan may have thought. She certainly didn't have the body that Caitlin had, if she did maybe she would wear a two piece. Ann didn't think Logan cared that she was wearing a modern take on a Marilyn Monroe classic swimsuit, Ann happened to love how the piece hugged her figure.

"So there I was having me morning cup of coffee and Logan there walks up. He's looking a bit haggard, so I hand him me mug and he takes this long slug," A wide grin breaks across Paddy's face as he continues telling the story, Ann enrapt in the words painting the Irishman's story.

Logan pulled Ann into his arms, her head naturally falling onto his chest in the tepid water of the hotel pool. He knew this story all too well, he was the one who took the infamous drink from Paddy's coffee mug in Iraq.

"Next I know he's coughing and sputtering coffee all over himself in the shop and everyone is looking at him. I'm laughing while he's turning red and choking." Paddy's infectious laughter carried over the two couples as Logan's skin flushed from embarrassment.

Logan pointed at Paddy, gathering attention to himself. "What this asshole fails to tell is that he drinks loaded coffee. How the hell he got a bottle of whiskey through customs and in country baggage checks is beyond me."

"Aye, a man never kisses and tells. It made me mornings brighter in hell though. Besides, ye seemed like ye was fine with it the next morning. Ye weren't so damned crabby working through the day." Paddy reached over to slap Logan's shoulder, a hearty laugh barking out around the group.

"Hell any time that a man could get a drink in that place was better than nothing. I think we finished that bottle off bit by bit. It lasted what, up to about a month ago or so?" Logan nodded in Paddy's direction, seeking clarification.

"Aye, you drank the last of it in that Coke I gave ye after they turned ye loose out of the CASH. Speaking of drinks, let's head on over to the bar and toss back a few what do ye say?" Paddy placed a chaste kiss on Caitlin's forehead, murmuring something in Gaelic into her hair.

Ann giggled as Logan planted his hands on her ass, easily hoisting her out of the pool onto the deck. He liked the look of her in the white Marilyn Monroe number, the sleek material hugging her curves. His thoughts turned to the dark side for a moment, before remembering that Paddy and Caitlin's clothes were up in the hotel room. There was no way he was going to be able to ditch them for the quickie that would result from getting Ann out of that swimsuit.

Logan followed Ann into the master bedroom, shutting the door behind them. His fingers deftly untied the bow laced around Ann's slender neck; Logan's lips kissing up her neck, nipping Ann's earlobe between his teeth. The throaty groan told him that Ann was thinking along the same lines he was, his body coming alive at the sound.

"Something you want Logan? If you do we got to be quick and quiet." Ann felt the evidence of his desire brushing against her ass, Logan was on board for that thought. Ann's arms came around behind her, wrists caught between one of Logan's large hands. His free hand jerked the damp swimsuit down her skin, the material scratching as it passed over her hips, pooling on the bedroom floor.

Ann looked back, seeing Logan stroking his hardening length, the hunger for her burning in his eyes. She blushed as Logan's free hand stroked up her back, pushing her face and chest into the bed. Ann felt the wetness seep into her folds, this man had no qualms about taking her hard and fast in the bedroom with their friends on the other side of the wall in the living room.

"Keep it quiet baby doll, I don't know if I can be gentle and quick." Logan's hands fell to Ann's hips, steadying the woman he loved on her feet.

"Just fuck me Logan. I need it, you need it." Ann surprised herself with the words that tumbled out of her mouth. Logan's eyes grew wide in astonishment. That was all the encouragement he needed, pressing into Ann without concern for Paddy hearing them. His strokes were laced with power, Ann's skin rippled under the punishment from Logan's hips. Every few strokes a gasp or squeak of pleasure would fall from her lips, her slick walls pulling him in deeper.

Fast minutes later, Ann felt Logan spasm deep within her, his head falling onto her back. Tender kisses peppered Ann's back, Logan's fingers snaking around her hip to tease the tight bundle of nerves at the juncture of her thighs. Ann buried her face into the bed, the groan muffled as she came undone under Logan. He could feel her body tremble underneath him, her chest heaving as she struggled for breath.

Ann rolled underneath Logan, pressing a kiss to his lips. "Jesus Logan, I was expecting that, but not like that." Her body responded in the same, as a full body shiver overtook her. She'd been fucked before, but nothing like that, not anything that bordered on primal. It was a lusty and exciting development in their relationship that was for sure.

A sheepish grin streaked across Logan's face as he pushed himself up from the bed, reaching down to pick up his swim trunks. He'd gone primal like that before on someone else long ago, but this moment with Ann was so much more restrained than what he had done in Guam.

"You in that swimsuit got me started, I had to finish it." Logan drawled, pulling on a pair of jeans over his naked hips. Ann sauntered over, watching the soft fabric of a button down shirt slink over his biceps.

A sweet smile graced her lips, her fingers trailing down the row of buttons, helping Logan dress. "Either way, I enjoyed every minute of it. Maybe something a little more drawn out than two quickies for later tonight?"

Logan smirked, knowing this was their last night together. "As soon as company leaves for the night, I promise you it'll be our time alone. We'll see how drunk you get at dinner and decide from there if you're getting any tonight."

Ann blushed watching Logan tuck the tail of his shirt into his jeans, knowing full well he wasn't wearing underwear. She was embarrassed, Logan had no idea just how much liquor she could put away before she was stumbling drunk. The last time she had been that drunk was the night of Krista's wedding, the night she'd slept with Dustin. Ann's cheeks paled at the memory of another man touching her, her stomach rolling in protest of the memory.

Concern painted Logan's features, his hands falling to Ann's bicep and hip. "You okay darlin'? Do we need to send company home and just order in and go to bed? You look like you don't feel so well all the sudden."

Ann waved Logan off, reaching for the dress hanging in the closet and a pair of panties in her bag. "It's nothing. We can go to dinner. I just need to get dressed." Ann slipped into the panties and dress, stepping over to Logan for help with zipping up.

"You sure you're okay?" Logan's voice cut through the silence like a knife, making Ann shiver.

"Yeah, I'm fine. It's nothing I promise. I'm pretty hungry after all that fun in the ocean and the pool. Let's get going please." Ann hastily brushed her hair out, tying it up in a ponytail.

"Yeah, can't leave them waiting anymore." Logan pulled on his boots, taking Ann by the hand and leading her out into the living room. His and Paddy's gaze followed their women down the hallway of the hotel and into the elevator.

Laughs abound through dinner, Logan loosened up with a few drinks in him, laughing along with jokes and stories flying around. His left hand rested protectively on Ann's thigh; she assumed it was instinctual, rather than territorial. Paddy's arm draped casually over Caitlin's shoulder, it was obvious they had something going on. Caitlin was a lucky girl to land the Irishman, he seemed to be the kind of guy who was a proverbial bachelor.

Paddy picked up the check for the dinner and bar bill, heading for the lobby of the hotel. Ann and Logan followed them out to the parking lot, finding a rental that looked similar to Ann's parked next to Logan's truck. The car looked small sitting next to the four wheel drive ranch truck.

Caitlin pulled Ann into a tight hug, "You take care of him. I don't want to have to patch him up again."

Ann nodded against the Corpsman's neck, "I promise, he's in good hands. Thank you for saving his life."

"Don't mention it. No greater love than that of a Navy Corpsman." Caitlin brushed a tear from Ann's cheek. "You'll be fine honey, trust me."

Logan and Paddy shared one of those awkward male hugs, before Paddy pulled Ann in for a bear hug. "We'll see ye soon. Ye need anything, ye got me number."

Ann took Logan's hand, watching as Paddy pulled out of the parking lot, heading towards the base. She knew Paddy would see Logan tomorrow, and knew if she needed anything he was just a text away. But that still didn't help the loneliness in her heart as the Irishman drove away.

"You look like you're about to drop, want to go up to bed? I promise you'll see him again, if I gotta bring him out to see you myself." Logan squeezed Ann's hand, seeing her startle at the reminder he was there. He knew where her mind was, it didn't bother him one bit.

"Yeah, let's go up to bed, gonna be a long day tomorrow." Ann's eyes sparkled in the moonlight as a smile brightened up her face. This was their last night together, they needed to make the most of it, with Ann's flight leaving in less than 18 hours bound for New York.

Chapter Twenty Nine

Ann brushed her damp hair straight before pulling it back into the customary ponytail she wore to bed. The soft brown tee-shirt Logan had sent her from Iraq hugged Ann's curves. Coming back up to the hotel room after saying goodbye to Paddy and Caitlin hadn't been without incident. Logan had stumbled getting out of the elevator, wrenching his knee in the process. Ann had called up for a bucket of ice, ensuring Logan was iced up and comfortable on the couch before she went to take a shower. As much as Ann would have liked spending her last night in California making love until the sun came up, she knew with Logan bumming his knee he wouldn't be feeling up to it. Logan meant more to Ann than sex, he was the whole package she had been looking for her whole life. Funny how fate played a hand in that, putting the card with his address in her hand.

Ann sighed as she shut off the light in the bedroom, her cellphone charging on the nightstand the only light in the room.

She hoped tonight she wouldn't sleep alone, passing the night lying in Logan's arms would mean more to Ann than anything. Although Ann understood the whole time difference thing a bit better now, as Paddy had explained it to her via text lying in that big bed alone, she still knew Logan needed to sleep. He couldn't go on with very little to no sleep anymore, as much as he may think it was okay. Humans had a certain threshold when it came to lack of sleep, crossing that threshold onto the other side produced not so favorable results. Ann knew first hand seeing some of the veterans doing sleep studies during her externship, it wasn't pretty. She hoped Logan never got that bad, it would break her heart to know something like what she had seen happened to him.

Her footsteps were silent on the plush carpet of the living room. The soft glow of the TV lit the room, Ann peered through the darkness to see Logan sprawled out on the couch. A soft smile graced her lips as she took in the sight of him, it was one of those moments that made a woman fall in love with a man. His left foot was propped up on the coffee table, a bag of ice laid across his knee on a towel. A bottle of Jameson with two short glasses sat next to his calf on the table, he knew what she liked to drink. Was it a guess or had she said something over the weekend about it? Ann couldn't remember, not that it mattered. What mattered was that Logan remembered a detail about her, which was touching.

Logan's dress shirt was pulled free from his jeans, with the buttons undone the wrinkled material laid open around his ribs, the ridges of his chest and abs rippling under Logan's skin as he breathed steadily. Logan's belt and buckle laid forgotten on the floor, his eyelids slits as the TV droned on in front of him. Ann stepped around the dark side of the couch, sliding under Logan's arm with a contented sigh. Logan startled before pulling Ann into his chest, her hand falling onto his abdomen, as the steady rhythm of his heart filled her ears.

Ann glanced over at the TV, seeing that Logan was watching an old black and white movie halfheartedly. She instantly recognized John Wayne and Susan Hayward, as the lead romance. Watching a bit more closely, Ann realized that John Wayne was wearing a Navy officer's uniform of a Lieutenant Commander.

"What movie is this? I recognize the Duke and Susan Hayward but no one else. I don't think I've seen this one before." Ann looked up into Logan's face, seeing his eyes glazed over. He'd probably taken some ibuprofen while she was in the shower, mixing it with the alcohol sped the drug through his system. Not something Ann the doctor would approve of doing, but something Ann the girlfriend wouldn't say anything about. Here with Logan she wasn't a medical student, here she was his girlfriend.

"The Fighting Seabees. It's kind of required watching when you're a Seabee. I've seen it so many times that I'm pretty sure I know it by heart. If you don't want to watch it I can change it. Just thought It was kind of cool that it was on TV, especially with all us coming home this weekend." Logan liked the feel of Ann breathing against him, the subtle scent of her shampoo easing his senses.

"No. Don't change it. I want to watch it with you. How much is left? Does it replay again later?" Ann was interested in a movie that was important to Logan and the Seabees. If she was going to continue this relationship they had, Ann needed to get familiar with the Seabee community a bit more.

"There's about an hour left. It doesn't come on again though. We can always go to bed after it's over. I want to get a goodnight's sleep tonight with you, so we can get up tomorrow and make the most of the last few hours we have together." Logan felt Ann burrow closer into his chest at the reminder of their timeline. He hated the idea of putting his woman on the plane back to New York after this weekend. If he had any say about it, Logan would take her back to Colorado with him and have Ann transfer to a medical school in Colorado. He was sure there was one in Denver, as much as he hated the thought of moving to the city, he could almost consider it to bring Ann home.

"Let's just watch the movie. I don't want to think about tomorrow yet." Ann felt the resounding rumble of agreement in Logan's chest. She didn't want to ruin the time she had left with him thinking about going home. That minute apartment in New York wasn't much, but it was only another year. If things worked out, maybe she could move out to Colorado next year after graduation and work at a hospital? Planning for the future was what dreamers did, Ann was more of a realist. Here and now was all that mattered.

By the end of the movie, Ann had cried herself into a snotty mess of emotions. Logan's bag of ice had melted, leaking into his jeans and onto the floor. Logan shifted Ann's weight so he could stand up, easily hoisting her into his arms. Her arms naturally came around his neck, with a slight limp Logan carried Ann into the bedroom. Setting her down on the bed, his hands glided up her sides, pulling the tee-shirt over her head. It didn't surprise him that she had nothing on under it but his dog tags. Ann had told him she slept in the shirt nearly the entire deployment. Logan watched Ann get comfortable, her gaze falling on the slight of his hips underneath the open shirt.

Logan stripped out of his clothes at the bedside, sliding into the cool sheets of the bed. Sleeping in the bed beat sleeping on the couch hands down, the bed was a helluva lot softer than the one he'd had in Iraq. His muscles turned fluid, his body instantly relaxing as the bed gave under his weight.

"Come here," Ann whispered, reaching over the side of the bed for her cellphone, pulling it free from the charger. Snuggling into Logan's neck, Ann positioned herself carefully, as to not reveal too much skin. Logan laced his arms around Ann, cradling her against his chest. Once she was satisfied that she wasn't going to be flashing anyone, Ann snapped a few photos of her and Logan in bed together. Logan didn't care that she took the pictures, but he was curious as to why. The pictures were clean, safe for work, anyone could see them, even Ann's parents.

"So why the pics sweetheart? Not that I mind, just curious as to why?"

"For when I wake up in New York from this dream, so that I know it was real and we were real. All of this feels like a dream, and I don't want to wake up if it is. What are we going to do after tomorrow? Are we over tomorrow or do you think we have a chance at something?" Ann's voice trembled, the thought of this just being a fling was too much to bear, especially after all they had been through. If they didn't try to make an honest go of the relationship, they would be lying to each other.

Logan blew out a breath, Ann's fears were valid. He'd seen a good bit of his guys draw out a relationship over distance through the years, just to have a piece of ass waiting on the flight line for them. The unsuspecting woman would be in love with the douchebag by the time he pulled in, and by the time the weekend was over she would never breathe his name again. It was all too common with some military guys. Some being the key word, Logan wasn't those guys.

"Hey now, we made it through the deployment. We're here now—together—in this bed. I'm not like some of the guys out there to fuck and chuck a woman. It ain't right. I want to try and make something more of this. But with me in Colorado and you in New York, it will be a bit of the same we'd been doing. Instead of an eight hour time difference it will only be two. We can call each other in the evenings when we're done for the day. I'm with you as long as you'll have me Ann. Promise you that."

Logan knew words were just that words. His actions after this weekend would prove to Ann that he was sincere. It would take the both of them to make it work, even with the distance cut down considerably. He had no problem of reconnecting his phone once he got back to Colorado. The first call he would make would be to Ann, proving to her that he meant every word he said.

"Thanks Logan. I still want to go out to the mountains with you, be with you. We'll just have to figure out when, I have to work out my school schedule and all. I'm glad you aren't one of those guys." Ann exhaled, pressing a tender kiss to Logan's lips.

"I can't be an asshole like that darlin', it just ain't me. You better now? Get you some sleep. We're getting up early to enjoy the day." Logan settled Ann into his side, where she belonged.

With his words Logan promised Ann to try and make a relationship. It didn't need to be a marriage or any of that. Just a promise. That was enough to settle Ann's heart and mind for the night. The warmth of Logan next to her was soothing, lulling her into sleep. Tomorrow she would enjoy the time left with the man she loved, no matter what happened.

Chapter Thirty

Logan woke with a stiff knee, other parts of his body reminding him of their solid presence with Ann tucked up against him. Tucking a lock of her hair behind her ear, he found she was still asleep. Not wanting to wake her, he eased himself out from under her before heading to the shower. Logan nearly jumped out of his skin when he pulled the shower curtain back to see Ann sitting on the bathroom counter. Striding over to her, Ann wrapped her legs around Logan's hips, pulling him into her. She breathed deep of the clean, woody scent that she knew was Logan. The smell of grease and oil wasn't as noticeable, but it was still there.

Logan pressed a kiss to Ann's neck, smirking at the breathless gasp he felt on his shoulder. This woman wrapped around him, he knew he loved her. He just couldn't say the words, not with how his life had been so far. Someday he could, but that day would be long coming.

"I need to get a shower, we need to get going." Ann moaned against Logan's shoulder, feeling him cupping her breasts.

"Mhmm. We got time." Logan slipped between Ann's folds, her heated wetness tight around him as he slowly rocked his hips.

Ann bit into Logan's shoulder, his swift motion of entering her hurt, but felt so good. With her head on his shoulder, Ann rode out the long moments of Logan thrusting into her. She found her rhythm late in the game, grinding her pelvis against his. The buzz gathering in her belly came quickly, Ann called out into the marble expanse of the bathroom. The orgasm soared around her, making her feel lightheaded as Logan pushed towards his release.

Logan grunted as his hand slapped down onto the smooth countertop. His strength left him as he made Ann his for the last time, his knees trembling under the adrenaline dump coursing through his body. His body shivered violently when Ann's fingertips brushed his neck and back.

Ann's deep blue eyes locked onto his, the emotions rolling through them like a storm out over the Pacific. Logan's heart hurt knowing this was the last time he would be with Ann like this for a long while.

"Logan, I love you."

"I know baby girl, me too."

Ann was satisfied with that reply, slowly sliding out from around Logan to get into the shower. They had half a day left together, there was no sense in wasting a minute longer.

Since there was a Seabee battalion coming in from deployment, with families meeting them on base, the Seabee Museum made special arrangements to be open on a Sunday. Logan knew Ann would enjoy learning more about the Seabees than he could tell her, the museum would be the perfect theatre for it. Wandering through the exhibits, Ann read placards about how the Seabees came to be from an idea of Rear Admiral Ben Moreell in 1941. He proposed Naval Construction Battalions to build and fight World War II. When the attack on Pearl Harbor brought the U.S. into the war, Moreell was given the nod and the Seabees were born. She found it amusing that the name Seabees came from the initials "CB" for Construction Battalions.

Ann's heart swelled realizing that Logan was part of a brotherhood that had ran strong for almost 70 years. These brave men and women signed their name to build airstrips, bases and other construction projects to benefit others. When the time came, they fought to keep freedom and others safe. She felt nothing but pride knowing the good the Seabees had accomplished worldwide throughout the decades. There were so many amazing exhibits of machinery, gear and things used by Seabees that Ann didn't realize just how much was really in the museum from what it looked like on the outside.

As they wandered through the exhibits, one exhibit caught Ann's attention. There was a photo collage of a young Seabee's boot camp graduation photo, the next series of photos were action photos of the young man working on projects with fellow Seabees. As the pictures flowed through, the second to last photo was a plane on a tarmac with a body on the ground underneath it. Ann's hear stopped in her chest as she read the accompanying placard, stating that Steelworker Petty Officer Second Class Robert Stethem was beaten, tortured and killed by Lebanese hijackers in 1985. His body was dumped onto the tarmac in Beirut, after being slain by the hijackers. Tears flowed down Ann's cheeks- this young man, not much older than her, had given his life to save the people held hostage on TWA Flight 847.

Ann jumped feeling Logan's hand grasp her own. The story of SW2 Stethem was one that every Seabee knew, he was awarded the Purple Heart and Bronze Star posthumously. Streets on the base that he and Ann were on had been named after the hero, as well as a destroyer that was currently operating in the Mediterranean Ocean in support of Operation Iraq Freedom. Logan carefully tugged Ann away from the exhibit and out of the museum. He was sure the reason why the exhibit hit Ann the way it did was because of his wound in Iraq, as well as Stethem being close to their own ages.

Logan pressed Ann against the fender of his truck, swiping his thumb underneath her watery blue eyes. He hated seeing her cry, especially knowing that something he had no control over caused her the pain.

"They murdered him. He was trying to keep those people safe and they murdered him and dumped his body like trash onto the tarmac. I don't understand how these terrorists can do things like that. How they can have no respect for human life. I don't get it Logan. Why?"

Ann sniffled, wiping her nose on the sleeve of Logan's shirt.

"Honey, that's just how some of them are. They're so brainwashed that they will kill Americans on sight and think nothing of it. Just remember that SW2 Stethem died a hero, and he will always be remembered that way," Logan took a deep breath before words he thought long forgotten tumbled from his lips.

"Lord, stand beside the men who build, and give them courage, strength and skill. O grant them the peace of heart and mind, and comfort loved ones left behind. Lord, hear our prayer for all Seabees, where'er they be on land or sea." The words trembled as they came automatically, words he last recited in unison with the battalion when they sent their fallen home from Iraq.

"What is that? It's beautiful." Ann gripped onto Logan's hand, squeezing gently. She had never heard the words before, but she could tell it was a prayer nonetheless.

"It's the Seabee Prayer. I don't know if you saw it in the museum, most of us know it by heart." Logan ran his thumbs over Ann's cheeks, evoking a small smile.

"You build, you fight. Every one of you are heroes in my book."

Logan shook his head slightly, seeing a frown paint Ann's features. "I'm not a hero babe, I'm just doing my job. Come on, let's get some lunch over at the NEX before I take you up to LA."

Logan opened the door for Ann, making sure she was belted in before closing the door. The diesel rumbled to life as they pulled out of the parking lot, heading towards the NEX.

Ann paired off inside the store to head to the restroom, Logan wandering through the shops near the ladies room, waiting for Ann to finish up. Ann found him standing in the line at Panda Express, trying to decide what he wanted to eat. Ann laughed at the look of concentration on his face as he decided, she never thought picking food was supposed to be such a chore.

The giggles didn't stop once they sat down to eat. Ann tried to stifle it with her hand as Logan mowed through his food with chopsticks, something she could never master. By the time Ann was halfway through her plate, Logan had finished his and was playing with the thin bamboo sticks in his fingers.

"Teach me?" Ann questioned, seeing the surprise creep into Logan's eyes.

"I can try, but not everyone gets it. It takes a good bit of dexterity in your fingers. Once you get it, it comes second nature. Here," Logan rose from his seat, stepping around behind Ann, taking the fork from her left hand.

Logan placed the two slips of wood in the correct position in Ann's fingers. Moving her fingers with his, he whispered how to do it in her ear. Within a few minutes Logan could see that Ann was catching on, slowly but surely eating with chopsticks. When he realized she was preoccupied with eating, Logan seized the moment to clasp a necklace around Ann's neck above the chain to his dog tags. The delicate gold chain draped her neck beautifully, Ann startled-- her hand dropping the chopsticks to grasp at her throat.

Ann ran her fingers over the pendant, figuring out the shape by feel. It was a Seabee, a choked sob caught in her throat. Logan kissed her neck, his breath tickling her skin.

"It looks beautiful on you from my vantage point." The rumble of his timbre held nothing but love for Ann.

Ann felt the tears welling up in her eyes, turning her head to kiss Logan fiercely. "Thank you Logan. I'll treasure it always."

"Glad you love it. We need to get going, got a bit of a ride up to LA yet still." Logan burned every moment into his memory, this was what would keep him wanting her to come home, the little moments like these.

Ann watched the ocean pass by as Logan maneuvered down CA-1 South. The view was a beautiful closure point to the weekend, she was sure Logan purposely chose it rather than the freeway. Her heart started to hammer in her chest as signs started to become more frequent for the exits to LAX. This was it, the last chunk of time they had together until whenever they could make their schedules work out.

Logan pulled into a parking space in the parking garage at LAX. He always hated goodbyes, but this wasn't goodbye. This was see you later, he had every intention of seeing Ann again. Helping Ann out of the truck, Logan pulled her close, breathing in the scent of her one last time. That subtle floral scent filled his lungs, reminding him of all the nights in Iraq that she lulled him to sleep without being aware of it.

Ann took Logan's hand in hers, his other hand rolled her suitcase along behind them. Ann watched as people came and went quickly, reminding her of JFK in New York. The city wasn't where her heart was, her heart was in Iraq, on the beaches of California and the mountains of Colorado. Wherever Logan was, her heart and her love was with him every step of the way.

Logan watched intently as Ann checked into her flight, pasting on a smile for the airline hosts as they handed over her ticket and directed her to the gate she needed. They walked hand in hand to security, both knowing this was it. Logan couldn't go any farther, as much as he wanted to. Thoughts of begging Ann to meet him in Colorado passed as quickly as they came, he wasn't that kind of man. If she loved him enough, she would find her way to him when the time was right.

Ann laced her arms around Logan, burying her face in his chest as the tears started to fall. She didn't want to leave, but there were so many loose ends she needed to tie up in New York before she committed to anything else. If Logan loved her like she thought he did, they would make the distance work.

"I don't want to go, but I know I have to. I promise I'll email you when I get home to let you know I made it okay. We'll figure something out about getting back together and doing that weekend in the mountains." Ann choked out, her tears staining Logan's shirt.

"I know you don't, and I don't want you to go. We'll figure it out, we always have. Looks like you got a long line to get through, baby." Logan knew he sucked at goodbye, he never could get the words right.

"Yeah, I know. Security sucks, takes forever to get through. Call me when you get back to Colorado?"

Logan grinned, trying to quell Ann's tears. "Promise you I will sweetheart. Ain't broke a promise to you yet have I?"

A bright smile broke through the tears as Ann chuckled, "Not yet. I gotta go you know."

Logan's reply came in a searing kiss that made Ann's toes curl. She gripped his biceps hard as he lifted her off the tile of the airport, not caring of the world passing by them. The world could have ended in that moment and Logan would have died a happy man. Ann was a bit unsteady when Logan set her down, blood coursing through her veins, gasping for breath.

Logan let go of Ann's hand, "I'll see you soon. This ain't goodbye." He could feel the tears forming in his eyes, but was too stoic to let them fall in front of her. He needed to be strong for her that was his job as her man.

Ann wiped at her eyes, taking hold of her suitcase and heading for the long line of passengers waiting to go through the security checkpoint. Taking her place behind an elderly couple in line, Ann looked back to see Logan watching her. His gaze burned across her skin, but her eyes transfixed on the movement of his lips:

"I love you, Ann."

A word from the desk of Riain-

Respectfully, CMC Dixon is the first in the Seabee Heroes series. The subsequent books will feature secondary characters from this book, as well as revisiting the main characters from this work. Look for *Mending Hearts* in 2015! Can you guess who that book will be about?

If you enjoyed reading this book, please leave a review of it where you purchased it, I love hearing from my fans!

Twitter- @Riainwacx

Riainwacx@yahoo.com

I do make mistakes, and my editor doesn't always catch me. Apologies if you caught me!

Riain Wacx

Respectfully CMC Dixon was started in January of 2014. It was completed through edits, designing, and final edits in June of 2014.

17142714R00232

Made in the USA
Middletown, DE
08 January 2015